LITTLE

LOST

GIRL

Book 1
Old Balmain House Series

Graham Wilson

BOOKS BY THIS AUTHOR

Children of Arnhem's Kaleidoscope – A Memoir

Old Balmain House Series

Little Lost Girl – Book 1

Lizzie's Tale   – Book 2

Devil's Choice – Book 3

Crocodile Spirit Dreaming Series

Just Visiting   – Book 1

Creature of an Ancient Dreaming – Book 2

The Empty Place   – Book 3

Lost Girls   – Book 4

Sunlit Shadow Dance   – Book 5

Reader Reviews of Old Balmain House Series

Amazon Reviews

★★★★★   Great Read

This is the story of three houses and the people who built them and lived in them from the mid-1800s to the present day. Told in a rather quaint and old-fashioned manner, it is a wonderful portrayal of a multi-generational family who lived through good times and bad, but always retained a strong family bond. The growth of this area seen through their eyes is fascinating. And, the mystery of Sophie's disappearance is enough to keep one reading

★★★★★   Wonderful books

I'm so glad I got all these books in a set. Each book reached further into the story, always going forward, but also bringing the past as the story unfolded. Well-written characters, and such detail that I felt I was walking alongside them as I read. No imagination is needed to see the people and places in your mind. Vivid descriptions brought the time and place to mind easily. Kindle said it would take more than 9 hours to read it. I did it over two days...I could not put it down! I've always dreamed of visiting Australia, and these books just increased that dream. Well worth reading!!!

★★★★★   Absolutely loved this series

Absolutely loved this series. I could not put it down, it has held me riveted to each story and looking for more. I could vividly imagine each tale and description of the places even though I haven't been there. I would recommend this collection to anyone who wants to read about the settlers in Australia passing through generations and the fast paced tale that goes with all the books in the collection. Well Done Graham Wilson. Can't wait to read the Crocodile Spirit Dreaming books now I have purchased them.

★★★★   Really enjoyed this story

Really enjoyed this story. Not so much historical Australian fiction out there. Made me go looking up the area online to see where they were talking about. It was sad and moved a bit quick through the characters at times but I thought it recreated the time period really well. Hard to imagine Sydney with that few people.

★★★★★   Five Stars

A brilliant read, very interesting

Barnes and Noble Reviews

***** I absolutely loved both stories

I highly recommend you get to read. Definitely looking forward to reading more by this author. Awesome!!!! Held my attention to the very end

***** A truly inspiring story, brought teams to my eyes

***** Wonderful

A beautiful story that will stay with me. Loved it and wanted it to continue. One of the best I have read lately.

***** Lizzys story

An amazing story, couldn't put it down. The author has written one of the best books I have read of this type. I was critical of the series he wrote at first but he had grown to be a favorite of min. A dramatic, fast paced, loving and exciting story.

***** If I could give it 6 stars I would!!!

It is not often a book will bring actual tears to my eyes but this one did as well as kept me up well past bedtime. If it does not touch you similarly I would be very surprised!!!

Kobo Reviews

***** Old Balmain House Book Series

Wonderful I couldn't bear to put them down.......wishing there were more in the series. The people were so real it's almost like I've met them.

***** Lizzies's tale

If we all had just some of Lizzies courage our world would be a much better place to live in. Such a nice story so interesting. Great read

***** A moving delight

A great story about a courageous young girl who triumphs despite adversity. The world needs more stories like this.

ACKNOWLEDGMENTS

I wish to thank the members of my extended family for information on our family's early history in Australia, particularly my Aunt Edith for passing on many stories compiled by others.

Many other people reviewed this novel in the four years since it was first published. Your advice, mostly positive, is greatly valued. Thank you all.

From readers reviews and a structural review by KJ Eyre, I have substantially revised this book and released a new edition It has many changes but keeps the main elements of the original story. Previously it was titled 'The Old Balmain House'. In doing this rewrite I realised the central story element is about a little girl and her friend who went missing and were never found. So I have changed the title of this book to 'Little Lost Girl'. The houses and other Sydney locations are important parts of the background, which give context and place the story. Hence the 'Old Balmain House Series' name keeps this sense of location within the story.

The new covers that accompany this second edition have been produced by Nada Backovic. I thank her for her creative flair in taking my descriptions of story elements and creating outstanding images which capture the story's moods and places. Arcangel Images supplied background images of the print versions of these books. The ebook images are designs of Nada Backovic.

Part of the inspiration for this book came from reading Geraldine Brooks novel, 'People of the Book', which used small artefacts of history to carry people's stories from the past into the present day. Geraldine also kindly gave me some suggestions for improvements for which I thank her.

CONTENTS

Author's Note

This is a work of fiction.

Balmain is a suburb of Sydney where we lived for seven years. Our house was like the cottage described in this book. We bought it as told here. Our pleasure living in it and in Balmain are real.

However, while many locations and parts of the history of Balmain are true, some locations and most characters are fictitious. For those interested, the factual information behind this story is in the Appendix at the end of the book. More information on Balmain and adjacent parts of Sydney is available from sources such as the Balmain Public Library, the State Library of NSW and the Balmain Association.

The purpose of this novel is not to merge fiction and historical fact, but to use some historical facts from Sydney's early development and a range of geographical locations around Sydney Harbour as a canvas onto which a work of imagination is painted. Parts of the canvas are known facts from my early family history, or the history of the area. These are like occasional dots of paint giving reference points and shadowed outlines. All the intervening layered detail to make this word picture has been created within my mind. If some parts approximate but differ from history or current reality, this is entirely accidental. I apologise if it causes offense through appearing to misrepresent true facts.

The idea which became this novel began soon after we purchased our much loved Balmain cottage. We discovered a sepia photo of a small girl who had lived in the house about 100 years ago. Later, in a writing class, I was shown an ornate perfume bottle, and asked to imagine a story based on it. I pictured it as the treasured possession of the girl whose photo we had found and jotted down headings for a series of scenes which told her story. Those points, imagined over five minutes, are now this novel. It is an imagining that I hope gives pleasure. This is the purpose of this book.

Family Tree – Main Characters

Rodgers Family

Archibald – Great Grandfather of Sophie – came to Australia from Scotland in 1841, builder of the first Balmain house, 'Roisin', in 1842

Hannah – first wife of Archibald – came to Australia in 1841, died in 1849, her children are James, John (deceased before coming to Australia, Archibald (deceased 1849), Alison, Hannah and Alexander

Helen – second wife of Archibald, children are Margaret (deceased 2 weeks after birth) Helen, (grandmother of Edith), Agnes and Anne

Alison – daughter of Archibald and Hannah, grandmother of Sophie, married Charles Buller

Maria – daughter of Alison and Charles Buller, mother of Sophie, wife of Jimmy Williams

Edith – (narrator's aunt), great granddaughter of Archibald Rodgers, through second wife, Helen

McVey Family

Tom McVey– Employer of Archibald and a family friend. Builder of the second Balmain house, 'Ocean View', in 1843

Mary – Wife of Tom, friend of Hannah, surrogate mother to Alison

Buller Family

John Buller – close friend of Archibald, joint business owner of Engineering Works in Sydney

Charles Buller – son of John, husband of Alison Rodgers, father of

Maria – mother of Sophie and wife of Jimmy Williams

Williams Family

Michael Williams –Welsh migrant, builder of 1870 Balmain house, 'Casa Ardwyn', father of Jimmy

Rosa –wife of Michael, daughter of Sophia, mother of Jimmy

Sophia –wife of ship's captain, Edward Martin, of Spanish descent from Philippines, mother of Rosa, grandmother of Jimmy

Jimmy – father of Sophie and Rachel, husband of Maria

Sophie –central character to story, born 1900, missing since 1908

Rachel– younger sister of Sophie

Sarah – daughter of Rachel, half cousin to narrator's Aunt Edith

Ruthie –aboriginal friend of Alison

Prologue

We bought ourselves a new old house – a magical timber cottage
It made us feel most welcome – gave a sense of a loving home
It seemed we belonged here – soon making it into our own
We glimpsed a hidden story – deep buried and held fast

It told about a little girl who lived here in a century past
This child went off to school one day and never did come back
It seemed to all who looked so hard she'd vanished through a crack
For years and years her family searched, seeking her elusive soul
Emptiness was all they found – she'd vanished and left a hole
Loss carried on, down years and years, as generations passed
The memory slowly dwindled, fading out of view at last

We heard her voice call out one day seeking help for her return
We joined the search; it drew us in, new people in this place
Across a century of time and space a presence led us on
At last we found a vital clue, lost story of her grandmother
And as we walked on hidden steps her family became our own
Now, at last, after all that's passed, we've safely brought her home

Chapter 1- A New Old House and a Discovery

We walked in and closed the door. This house was ours. The agent's brochure said it was built around 1870. We wondered about its story and how it had come to be here?

We had lived in Balmain just over a year, coming here by accident. Arriving in Sydney, five years earlier, we were agog at the real estate prices in Australia's biggest and busiest city. So, at first, we rented a house in Sydney's suburban south from owners away in Singapore. Their son was injured. Unexpectedly, they returned to Australia. We needed a new house to live in. Marie, my wife, worked in the city. My job would move there soon too. So a move to inner-city Sydney made sense.

With little time before we had to move we looked at houses to rent in the inner suburbs of Newtown, Camperdown and Glebe, just south of the city. Most were terrible; dirty bathrooms and kitchens, busy streets and little space. I saw a listing for a townhouse in nearby Annandale with four bedrooms. My inner-west Sydney internet search had also brought up a four-bedroom townhouse in Balmain, although it was $70 a week more than the Annandale one. Thus far I had left Balmain out of consideration. I thought it was too expensive and only trendies lived there. However, with little time to find a house for three children, we added Balmain to the list.

We visited both properties. The Annandale one was next to a park, along the local creek. It was one of three buildings in the small complex. We liked it. So I made an offer of $20 less than the advertised rate. The Balmain property was spacious, but in large complex and the extra $70 a week was real money. However, to cover ourselves, we decided to make an offer for this too, at $50 less than asked, to give us bargaining room.

Next day the phone rang. It was the Annandale agent, saying they would rent us the house, but would not accept a reduced price.

I said, "Sorry, that's our offer."

A second later I wondered if I should have taken it.

Five minutes later the phone rang again, this time the Balmain agent. They would rent us the house and our offer was fine. We agreed, headed off to sign the papers and pay the deposit. Five minutes later the house phone rang again. We were gone so it went to message. That night we heard this message from the Annandale agent saying their client reconsidered and agreed to rent us the house at our nominated price. Too late; money paid and form signed for the Balmain rental.

Two weeks later the move to Balmain was made. I hate moving more than almost anything else, but by the end of the day we were in, just; boxes everywhere, partially assembled furniture; our legs like jelly from endless trips up and down three flights of stairs. But the house was clean, seemed comfortable and gave us a pleasant home for now.

After a minimal dinner we set out, with our children, to explore our new neighbourhood. It was dusk light of a spring day. By this time, in our previous suburban house, the streets were empty; everyone retired inside, settled in front of TVs for the night.

Here streets were alive; others like us out on an evening walk, people from every second house spilling out onto the footpaths, chatting with neighbours, patting dogs, dodging kids or just taking in the night air. It did not feel like suburban Sydney but like a village where everyone was a part. For Marie, from an Irish village, she had found a place where she felt at home, a village of people who came together in public spaces, like tens of thousands of European villages.

By the time we finished our walk it was decided. We loved this place. We would buy a house here. As the weeks passed and we settled into Balmain everything reinforced our desire to live in this place. It was a suburb full of history; one of the first parts of Sydney settled when the colony was founded, the next peninsula jutting into the harbour west of the city. It was a five minute ferry ride to the city, passing under towering Sydney Harbour Bridge. It was full of wonderful places to visit and explore, old stone houses built into hillside nooks looking out across the harbour, grand terrace houses and little workers cottages, wonderful shops and restaurants, lots of pubs with an authentic local feel and many older people who had lived here all their lives, people with their innumerable stories who kept alive a spoken history of this place.

So we began to look for a house of our own. There was not much for sale, at least not much we could afford. Years of real estate boom did not buy a lot of house for your money in inner Sydney. We sold another property we owned. That gave us a deposit, and the interest rates were rising, so perhaps, perhaps, that would help.

Four months into the lease of our Balmain townhouse the agent rang to say that, unfortunately, the owner needed to sell. He was an over-geared victim of rising interest rates which kept going up. So we needed to find a new place to live. We had not found anything to buy but would not to be rushed; so another move was needed, but only within Balmain. This time we rented a grand terrace in East Balmain, looking out towards Sydney Harbour Bridge. Now, used to Balmain prices, it only cost us an extra $70 a week, which seemed fine. It had million dollar views of the boats on Sydney Harbour and Marie could catch the ferry to work.

Then we found it, or actually Marie did. It was about the tenth house we looked at in three months, a shabby double fronted weatherboard cottage. It was built on a large level block, clad in the wide timber boards of a hundred years past. It had the feel of a well built house, well proportioned, though showing its age. It was painted a softened lemon yellow and had a twisted old frangipani tree in the front yard. Across the street, with ridge-top city and harbour views, were the grand terraces and other fine houses of the wealthy, all built around 1870-80. Our street side had houses of ordinary people, mostly two bedroom weatherboard cottages, some renovated and extended; others like ours standing almost unchanged for over 130 years.

Marie rang the agent inquiring, who said, "Unfortunately an offer has been made and accepted, so it's too late."

It seemed our search must continue.

Two days later we saw this same house advertised again.

Marie rang back. She was told the bidders had money problems so it was back on the market.

We rushed for an inspection. The house had great bones but a declining air; grand original fireplaces and ceilings; awful mouldy old brown carpet and a collapsing chipboard kitchen. However, the moment we stepped inside, it exuded a positive feeling, like a welcoming relative – come in, enjoy me, I am a good place to live; I like you and know you like me too!

Within five minutes we decided to make an offer, near the upper limit of what we could afford. The agent said there was already a conditional bid in from another party, but this person needed a few days to get their finance sorted out before they could confirm.

We placed our bid. The agency said they would put our bid to the owner, but thought we needed to go higher. They promised to ring us next day, once they had talked to the owner.

So we waited and hoped. Next day the agent rang back. The owner was keen to sell and, having been burnt once, was not inclined to wait for the other bidder. But the listing price was $30,000 above our offer, so we needed to close the gap to get favourable consideration. A deep breath; another ten thousand went onto the table for the agent to put to the owner. Five minutes later the phone call came – offer accepted, the house was ours.

***

It was February when we moved in. We collected the keys from the Balmain agent's office and drove to the front door.

A balmy summer's day wafted a fragrant scent from the ancient knurled frangipani tree in the front yard. A decrepit picket fence stood barely holding back an escaping garden. It sprawled over the path we followed to the front door. We walked under a rusty tin roofed verandah sheltering weathered floorboards. On the front door a tarnished old iron knocker sat above a small metal plate, aged and corroded, faintly inscribed *'Casa Ardwyn'*.

The key turned; we were inside. It really was ours. The house exuded shabby charm. Many people had lived here. Most felt good. But sad memories intruded too. What had it seen in 130 years of history?

We started to unpack and bring order to our new old house. The back garden was overgrown with straggly shrubs below a massive gum tree, it's trunk a metre across. It must have lived here, shading the local aborigines, before the First Fleet came. Other big trees competed for space in a crowded canopy. A previous owner built a deck extending under the trees, giving filtered summer sun on balmy days. We sat out there for half an hour, soaking it in, while our resident magpies and kookaburra gave melodic voice.

Our daughter had the front bedroom across the passage from us. Our boys had the attic in the roof cavity above our head. We busied ourselves with organising our parts.

"Mum and Dad, look what I have found." The voice drifted across the passage. Our daughter, Tara, aged eight, came into our room carrying a shiny glass thing in her hand.

"What is it?" we both asked together.

She shrugged and said, "Looks like an old bottle," handing over her discovery. A small, blue-green glass bottle, covered with silver lace filigree in which a blue stone sat, and with a silver screw top, colour tarnished dark with age, perhaps a perfume bottle of another time.

"Show us where you found it," I asked.

She led us into her room to where an old ornate fireplace was. "I was looking here and put my hand in here," she said, pointing to the fireplace, and then, indicating to the bottle, "I felt this thing, it seemed to pull my hand to touch it. I wonder if I should put it back?"

However curiosity had the better of me. It was as if this bottle had called out to be discovered, this first find in our new house.

I took the bottle from my daughter's hand. Despite being cold glass it felt warm to touch. I rolled it in my fingers to examine it, such delicate silver lacework, now tarnished with age, a patina of time toned to a soft lustre. One small blue stone was set into the silvered side, perhaps a piece of coloured glass, perhaps a valuable gem. The bottle glass was the colour of a milky summer tropical sea, as seen at the edge of the shoreline where colours of trees, sea and sky flow through each other; between opaque and translucent, a mixing of blues and greens.

I opened it, curiosity piqued. It appeared empty but I saw a faint residue, remains of 100 years past. I put it to my nose. The faintest perfume rose to meet me; apples, cinnamon and gum leaves, blended with summer breeze and frangipani. Unbidden, thoughts of other times and places flowed through my mind, as if hundreds of souls brushed past with the gentlest touch. I must have been smiling because Tara and Marie both asked why.

So I passed on the bottle. Each described special scents and memories it evoked in them, different but similar. I felt a desire to know more.

I found a torch to light the cavity. Tara squeezed her head into the small gap where the fireplace finished and the chimney started.

"There's something else in here" she said.

She pulled out an oval silver frame. It held a faded sepia photo of a small girl, age similar to herself. Written on the back, in neat but faded writing, was 'Sophie, 1900-1908'.

It and the perfume bottle had been resting on a half brick ledge, about an inch wide, above the fire place at the start of the chimney. It seemed that here they stayed, waiting while a century passed, waiting for another little girl to come. Then they called to her to be discovered.

Tara looked at the photo intently. "She looks nice; I wonder what happened to her?"

Marie said, "I think she must have lived here and died when she was about as old as you. Perhaps she got sick and her Mummy and Daddy left her perfume bottle and photo here to remember her by."

Tara looked dubious for a moment then her face brightened.

"I think you're right. She wanted me to find these because she was like me. She wanted me to find them to remember her."

I took the photo from Tara and looked more closely at this small girl who had summoned my daughter in her own way.

A girl in a white lace dress;

"First Communion dress", my Catholic wife, Marie, said.

I searched this child's face, framed by dark hair. Gazing at those eyes from over 100 years ago, it felt like she was staring back at me, staring right into my soul, linking to my mind: child eyes with a touch of mischief; but yet so serious and so knowing; a soul born wise.

I sensed a tenuous thread reaching out, coming to me and my daughter, a gossamer touch from beyond the grave. It was a transfer across space and time, an eerie and almost familiar connection. It felt as if a long lost spirit had called out to me. Goosebumps rose on my arms and I shivered.

I wondered who she was and what was her story? I felt drawn to find something out about her, the girl child in the photo frame.

Chapter 2 - Investigation

We settled into our new house. I googled the door name plate 'Casa Ardwyn'. Casa was Spanish for house or home; Ardwyn was the Welsh word for 'house on a hill'. It seemed a good name for our house, a home built on the crest of a hill, with glimpsed views to a distant harbour and city. Perhaps its builder had Welsh and Spanish heritage.

There was much work to be done to make this house liveable; repainting of walls and floors, new cupboards, a rebuilt kitchen and bathroom. So, over coming months, we painted and cleaned, we did the simple repairs needed and transformed the garden. When our friends and our children's friends visited, all commented about how pretty it looked and what a good feel it had. We agreed. It was our house; it felt good, we loved it and it gave the good back.

We had our vision splendid of extending our small cottage out around the garden, but first we needed to work, save, and pay down our purchase mortgage debt. Then, in time, this dream may happen.

A year passed.

One day I was in the Mitchell Library in Sydney City doing other work. The discovery of the perfume bottle and girl's photo popped into my mind. I told the librarian our family had bought an old house in Smith St, Balmain. I wanted to find out its history and particularly about the people who lived there around the turn of the last century, as we had found a photo of a girl in the house dated 1908.

The librarian thought for a second and said, "You will probably have to go to a few places. We have some early records here and there is also material with the Balmain Historical Association, the National Library and the various registries like the Land Titles office and the Registry of Births, Deaths and Marriages.

"Perhaps you should start in our archives and see what you can turn up for Balmain around the time the house was built and also for the period in the early 1900s. You could look at old newspapers from that time and see what stories come up; they might explain some of what was happening then. Things such as whether there were any major new buildings or local events, and any other things which happened, like new schools being opened, major accidents or epidemics which affected the local population."

So I started with the Sydney Morning Herald Archives as they were most convenient. I picked the year 1908 and started on the January papers. There were lots of stories about important people coming and going, the crowding and disease in Sydney docks and the early politics of Federation. I came across a series of stories about the bad blood between the teams in the rugby competition, with an announcement to set up a new code called 'Rugby League', the first game was to include a Balmain team and be played at Birchgrove Oval.

In early September, 1908, I found something interesting. It was about the disappearance, two days earlier, of a boy and girl from Balmain. The report was dated September 5th, making the disappearance date September 3rd. The girl's first name was Sophie. Both children had been at school and had left together, a couple hours after lunch, when school finished for the day. That was the last time they were seen. The previous day a widespread search was done with the police and over 100 members of the community, but no trace had been found. The search was hindered by heavy rain on the night of the disappearance that washed away any tracks or scent.

The paper told of two lines of speculation; that the two children, who were close friends, had run away together and the possibility of foul play, kidnapping, or other similar things.

It told too that a large sailing boat had been moored just off East Balmain on the day of the disappearance and had set sail in the mid afternoon. Was it possible that the two had stowed away on this?

Several boat loads of disreputable sailors had been visiting Balmain on that day, going to the local taverns. About half had sailed the next day. Could one of these sailors have something to do with the disappearance? The day after several sailors from the drinking party in Balmain on the day the children went missing were located and questioned both by the police and the newspapers. All denied knowledge of these children, though it was obvious that some had been very intoxicated and remembered little.

Over the next week a few additional small articles emerged. The parents were adamant their children would not run away, but the whole of Balmain had been thoroughly searched over the week, without trace, and there was nothing to suggest foul play. Both children were very independent and each had been in trouble that morning. So the considered opinion was moving towards an absconding explanation.

But really it was a mystery. Inquiries would be made at the ports of destination of boats that left the harbour on the day of the disappearance and on the next day, to see if anything had been seen of the children on these departed ships.

With this the story faded away. Three months later, in early December, I found a notice in the paper. It told of a joint prayer meeting, involving St Augustine's Catholic Church and St Andrews Presbyterian Church in Balmain, encouraging parishioners to attend church to say special prayers of intercession for the safe return of Mathew McNeil and Sophie Williams, of Smith St Balmain.

Now I was now almost certain that the girl in our picture was Sophie Williams and that she, along with her friend, Mathew McNeil, had gone missing and not been found after three months. But here the trail vanished.

I was left with a faded photo, a delicate blue green glass bottle, along with two children's names, as parts of a mystery.

Chapter 3 - 1841 - Arrival in Australia

There was a smell of burning in the air as the boat came in to the wharf in Cockle Bay. After months of sailing out from a cold, dreary Scotland, bright light bouncing off the rocks and water in this sheltered bay, combined with wisps of smoke from headlands on the north side of the harbour, was his first real view of this strange land. To the east was Port Jackson where they had berthed briefly late last night. Some people had come off there, but Sydney town was crowded with no space to stay tied up in Campbells Cove. So most passengers stayed on board as the harbour pilot directed them around the headland to a sheltered bay, to anchor and unload the next day.

Archibald stretched his cramped muscles and walked around the deck in the early morning of October 5th. A slight chill was in the air, but with bright sky and the promise of a warm day to come. His home, in Barnyards village, Scotland, would be damp and misty on a day like today, but some of his heart yearned for its comfortable familiarity. His wife and their two small children slept on in their cramped quarters. He tasted the early morning ocean breeze; sea brine, shellfish, gum tree and wood smoke, all mingled.

Cockle Bay Wharf was already bustling. Merchants with carts sought to unload supplies; boats jostled for space to tie up on these crowded wharves. Extending from shore was a forest of masts and canvas which rocked gently in the swell, with sounds of creaking hulls and the squawk of birds.

To the west, perhaps half a mile away, was another headland, mostly covered in grey-green trees, but with patches of clearing towards its end and some houses, newly built. As he watched a small boat headed out from that shore and rowed steadily across the gap, before disappearing around the headland to the east. Sitting in the back was a distinguished-looking, suited gentleman, while two oarsmen pulled him steadily across the water.

Now that seems to be a good place to live and a good way to get to work, Archibald thought, as he contemplated the view across the sparking water. It was so different from work in his poor country village in Scotland, moulding metal implements over a forge in a smoky barn, with muck and mud and grey skies outside.

A new life was in front of him. What would it hold? Anticipation mingled with the regret of no longer seeing his six brothers and sisters and his worn parents in their small hillside cottage. Not much future there. Still he missed the small grave for John, little Archibald's twin brother. They had dug it into the hard frost, on a cold day of last winter, looking down across the loch. It was this event, more than any other, that prompted the leaving.

As the early morning passed into full day, Archibald negotiated for a man with a cart to haul his furniture, tools and other bulky goods to a store shed behind the wharf.

He left Hannah, with their children, on-board and went off, walking up to the town. He found a boarding house with a spare room in George Street. They could stay here for a few days until he found something better.

It was amazing how alive the town was, they said it had now passed 40,000 people. That did not seem a lot after England and Scotland, yet there were crowds pushing along George Street, and lots of redcoat soldiers and convicts in work gangs. Everywhere was noise, dust, flies and a stench of unwashed sweat, horses and manure.

It all seemed incredibly alive and busy with industry. The buildings ranged from sandstone and brick houses, built over two and three levels, to little more than timber hovels, particularly on the side streets. Gradually he came towards Semi-Circular Quay, where they had berthed last night. Here the order increased, crowds thinned out and fine buildings of local sandstone were more numerous.

Archibald was captivated by the vitality of it all, all these people, free settlers, soldiers, emancipists and convicts, all trying to make a life for themselves and seeking their own advantage. Everything seemed to cost a lot, but it was definitely a place of opportunity. Then, realising that the day was running away and they had much to do, he returned to the ship.

Soon it was time to leave the *'William Turner'*, their home coming over the water for four months. They loaded their luggage onto a cart and were driven away from the boat, wheels clanking on the rough wharf decking.

The Customs man checked them and wrote their names in his log book;

'Archibald Alexander Rodgers, aged 27, Black Smith, Presbyterian, can read and write;

Hannah Rodgers, aged 24, Dressmaker, Presbyterian, can read and write.

Children: James aged four and Archibald aged two.'

The Customs man watched them drive away, thinking, *this tall, dark haired, almost saturnine, man and his pretty, fair haired wife, with the sunlight smile, but also with quiet competence; they would be two who did well in this colony.*

Hannah and the children stopped at the boarding house while Archibald went off, needing to look for work as they had little money left after the trip.

Someone told him that they were looking for iron-workers at McVey's, on Mace's Wharf in Sussex Street. He wrote directions on a scrap of paper and walked the half mile there. Sure enough, anyone who could work metal was wanted, lots of ships needed repairs and people were looking for cart wheel repairs and iron implements for farming and building.

It was past midday on Friday so he said he would like to go to church on Sunday and come back to start on Monday.

Mr McVey, proprietor, replied, "Well, I would think you'll be looking for the Presbyterian Church then. I will see you there on Sunday morning and introduce you to the other parishioners. We are just a wee flock yet, but we try to help each other. Call me Tom."

Weeks in Sydney soon passed. Archibald struck up an instant friendship with Tom McVey, who reminded him of his father with his

Scottish brogue and manner; a grizzled man, now moving into his fifties, with years of hard living starting to show; but still a tireless bull of a man, with corded muscles built up from years of hard labour in the engineering firm.

Archibald's work was often back breaking, casting and moulding ships fittings and building tools for the frenetic activity around the town, but his years in the forge in Barnyards had given him stamina and a capacity for hard work. Often he was last to leave, his pride insisting that he finish all his jobs. However, the money was good and they lived frugally so, suddenly, they had some small savings.

Sunday was a day of rest. They had become expected visitors for lunch at McVey's, after church, at their house just behind the shipyard. Two of the McVey children, the older sons, had returned to London and married there, and the youngest, a boy around Archibald's age, had disappeared on a voyage five years ago. So it felt like they were adopted as a new set of children, with James and Archibald Junior as favourite grandchildren, spoiled and their antics much loved. Mary McVey looked with fondness on their blond heads, so like her own children of two decades before and the grandchildren she almost never saw in London. Without a daughter of her own Hannah seemed the daughter she had never had.

Mr McVey had found them two small rooms with a share kitchen in a tenement near the Engineering Works, but Sydney Town was crowded and good places were hard to find. Hannah was expecting another child and they would need somewhere better soon.

One day, over Sunday lunch, Mrs McVey broached the subject. "Have you made any plans about a place of your own?"

Archibald and Hannah exchanged glances. It was something they had talked about with no solution. Their meagre savings still would not extend to building their own house further out and, with the long hours of work, it would be hard to move too far away. Still, it was getting hard to live with an exuberant two and four year old in two small rooms and there was no place for children to play in the busy, crowded city streets. And now, with a baby growing inside her,

Hannah was often tired. She was making dresses to sell in her spare time, to earn extra money, but this was getting harder.

Without waiting for an answer Mrs McVey plunged on. "Tom and I, we have been thinking, blocks are for sale across the water in that new suburb they call Balmain. We know ye don't have the money yet, but we know you will soon, the way you work at the yards, Arch, not to mention all the extra hours Hannah finds to make dresses when these two rascals let her."

Tom came in, "You need to have a look yourselves first to see if you like the place, but if you do, I could advance you the money to buy a block of land over there. You can pay me back from your wages over the next year. How about next Sunday we all go over there for a look? Then you can decide if you think it is a good idea."

The following Sunday, as he got out of bed, Archibald realised Hannah was already up, working busily in the kitchen. He came quietly up behind her and put his arms around her waist. She jumped at his unexpected presence, almost dropping the tray of buns she was taking from the oven.

"Mm, they smell good! You have been busy, are they for our breakfast?" he said, reaching out as if to grab one.

Regaining her balance, Hannah slapped his hand away. "No you don't you greedy thing, these are for lunch. Yesterday, while you were at work, Mary and I made plans for a picnic in Balmain today, when we go over to look at the land. You hadn't forgotten had you?"

After church they all headed down to the shipyard where Tom had a boat waiting. James and Archibald Junior perched on the front, Tom and Archibald each took an oar and Mary and Hannah sat in the stern.

Archibald could not help but catch the infectious excitement of his boys, at this, their first outing away from Sydney Town and on a row boat. What could be better than a trip on this beautiful harbour?

He remembered his first morning, watching the suited gentleman rowing across from the headland just to the west. He realised now this was the place they called Balmain. Until now it had been only a distant grey-green rocky shore and a name. For a minute, after they pushed off, he and Tom bent their backs to the oars. Soon they had a good rhythm going and were flying over the water, little waves slapping against the bow and the boys cheering with excitement at each splash.

After a few minutes Tom stopped rowing and said, "Rest up a second, Arch. Have a look at where we are going."

They sat there, like a tiny cork bobbing in a bath, while Archibald surveyed the scene. A few hundred yards behind them already, the Sydney shore was fading into a view of masts and sheds, with the land rising up behind them to the town. Ahead was a low scrubby peninsula of land, Balmain. It was a place with grey-green trees and jumbled boulders, many big sandstone slabs like those being quarried to build the fine houses and the public buildings of the town.

Tom pointed out landmarks. "See the mills on the hill, Sydney side, that's why they call it Millers Point. Further round there you can see that fine house and the gun battery, that's Dawes Point; on the other side of it is Semi-Circular Quay and there, sitting in the middle of the harbour, out from Balmain, is Goat Island, where they kept a mad convict chained for years"

Then he turned his attention back to the land in front. "See that timber jetty a few hundred yards away, that's Balmain wharf. Most houses are built behind it though I hear they have started work on a new town centre about a mile back. There is a rough cart track from the wharf going up there but now the convicts are building a better road. It must be hard going for them with all the rocks and gullies. You can see it's only a short way across here by water but it's a long trip around by horse; five miles by road rather than half a mile by boat."

Soon they pulled up to the shore, tying the boat to a rough hewn timber jetty with big tree posts to hold it up. It looked strong enough to withstand a wild winter storm. They left the wharf and went in single file up the path. It was a narrow way, winding between gaps in the boulders. To the right there was a cart track, gradually coming up where the slope was gentler, but their path went straight up.

For Archibald and Hannah it was so strange, a land of opposite seasons, summer now with bright harsh light when their home was winter; grey rain, heather covered hills swathed in mists which swept up from the firth, and hard frosty days with low slanted light reflecting off the loch as the sun tracked briefly in an arc just above the horizon.

Here was a land which smelt of gum, and now, as the morning heat rose, it gave off a smell of dried out leaves and dead grass. Prickling them on the path were sharp grasses, spiky twisted leaves and odd shaped twisted cones, something which Tom said was called Banksia, named after that redoubtable scientist, Joseph Banks.

Tom carried little Arch on his shoulders and Hannah walked behind, almost side by side with Mary, while Archibald enjoyed the boy chatter of young James, who marvelled at every new discovery, the ants and beetles on the path, bright feathered birds called parrots which swept through the trees with a raucous squawk. Half way to the ridge was a flat place on the hillside, towered over by a giant fig whose roots made huge projections out from the trunk and across the ground.

Here they sat for a minute, in eye resting shade, and felt sweat prickle their skins in the late morning heat. A raucous laughing sound erupted from high above in the trees. Archibald and Hannah looked up, alarmed, then glanced at each other for reassurance.

Tom, noticing their concern, laughed. "Don't worry about that, it catches everyone first time, it's the laughing jackass, kookaburra as some call it, see that blue-brown bird and its mate high in the foliage above. They call to each other in that strange laughing sound. Soon it will be so familiar you will barely notice. They are great birds for killing snakes; that is something you will have to watch out for in this hot weather with the two lads. The snakes here are bad ones, with a poisonous bite that kills people, some use a dog to keep them away though often the dog gets bitten and dies. The best thing is to make plenty of noise so they hear you coming and get away."

They walked on, now with eyes glued on the path, to avoid snakes lying in wait. Tom could not help a grin as he watched the seriousness of the novices. As they reached the crest of the path there was a sudden thump-thump in front. Running alongside the path, heading across a clearing, ran two furry animals, with a hopping gait. They looked like a small type of the kangaroos that they had seen in story books of Australia.

Hannah pointed in excitement while little Arch and James screamed, "Kangaroo-Kangaroo".

Mary laughed, saying, "That's just a rock wallaby, you see plenty around here, mostly kangaroos live further out, on the other side of Parramatta, in places where there are good open grasslands."

Up on top of the hill the land opened out. There were patches where the trees were cut down, some with new built houses and others with pegs to mark boundaries. Tom led them east, along the ridge, where the best view across the water to Sydney Town was. It was seen as a sprawl of distant buildings, covering a promontory; some grand houses, others just shacks.

Tom pulled out a map he had brought and said, "I think there are some vacant blocks around here, Lots 406 and 407 should be nearby. Soon Tom found a peg in the ground, showing the corner of one. It was level ground with a low lip of loose boulders, and a half screen of banksia trees rising near the edge, before it fell away to the water.

Hannah came over to Archibald and took his hand. "Isn't this a perfect place for a picnic?"

She noticed Tom looking at his map and pointing to the peg. "This is one of the blocks I thought you might like, sheltered just behind the ridge and with a great view from the edge back across to Sydney town. See over there, you can just make out our shipyard."

Hannah, flushed from the climb, fair hair tied back from her face, looked at Archibald with eyes of wonder. "Do you think we could buy one of these? It is beautiful; I love the way the light filters through the banksia trees and how the view from here opens to the harbour before us."

Archibald, caught in the enthusiasm of the moment, found himself smiling back at her. As their smiles touched, he heard himself say. "Well, I think that is what Tom here is saying, that these ones are for sale and he will stand us the money till we can pay it back. So, while I hate taking what I don't own, if that's what you want then maybe we should buy it."

James and Archibald Junior broke the conversation as they came rushing over pointing. "Da, Da, there is a big creature in the bush there."

Archibald took the two small hands of his sons and walked towards the pointing. He did not see anything for a minute in the broken dappled light of the bushes at the edge of the clearing. Then his eyes clicked into sharp focus. There was a huge lizard, more than a yard long, stretched out on the ground under a bush, watching them with small beady eyes and slowly flicking out and drawing back its tongue.

Tom, following close behind, suddenly saw it too. "What a beauty, an old man goanna, the aborigines really like them to eat, especially when they are good and fat like this one. Now that most aborigines have left here to camp near the end of the bay it seems they are getting common again."

It was time for lunch. They all sat on a rug in the shade and ate fresh buns, sliced meat and accompaniments. From where they sat at the edge of the ridge they could watch the boats come from Cockle Bay around the point. Suddenly they would catch the breeze which swept up the harbour, heeling over as they rounded Dawes Point.

As they sat, eating, a breeze off the harbour came sweeping up over them. It washed away the heat of the still morning. "Ah," said Tom, "the blessed relief of that first breath of the afternoon sea breeze. Normally it comes up about now in summer, rising up and over these headlands, and making for a cooler afternoon."

Tom turned to Archibald, saying, "Well, what do you think? Do you like the idea of living here?"

Archibald felt awkward. These kind people had done so much for them. He felt greatly in their debt. It cut against his Scottish ways to take what he had not already earned. But he knew Hannah loved it and he could feel it was right for him and their children too.

He hesitated, not sure what to say. As he paused two little blue birds came fluttering out of the bushes and down amongst them, searching for crumbs, beautiful blue flashes of light on their iridescent wings, so tiny you could hold one in each of your palms. One hopped over, standing next to him. It looked up, surveyed him intently with tiny eyes and bobbed its head three times, as if saying this was a good place for them all to be in. Just as suddenly it flew away, its brilliant blue flashing wings, lighting the sky. It seemed a good omen for living here. Archibald found he was unconsciously nodding his head in agreement.

Tom continued on "If you keep your jobs up on other days, why don't you finish early on Saturdays. Then you can come over here and get to work building your own house. In fact, when we have a quiet day, I could get a few of the boys to come over to help. I reckon if we all get to it we will soon have something built. There is plenty of spare timber that you can start with in the yard, all those planks from those machinery packing crates we just bought in for starters."

Archibald and Hannah felt stunned at this generosity. Before they could reply Mrs McVey came in, "Well, right then, it's all settled. Not that you said yes, too proud for that, but you did not say no either. We know you'll do well with it, so that's it."

All they could do was stumble out some thanks.

Summer moved into autumn. By autumn their first Balmain house was built, a room for them, a room for the children, a room to sit in with a table and chairs, a kitchen and wash house out the back, and a shaded verandah at the side, where they could sit and look across the water to the windmills on Millers Point. It seemed so grand after what they had had. On the day when the nailing of the boards was finished, Archibald brought Hannah over to look at the finished structure.

She said, "It's well done and it's grand. Now all we need is a name." She cast her eyes around, thinking aloud. "Perhaps I will grow some pink and yellow roses to ramble over the outside, a bit of the old of Scotland to sit alongside the new. Roisin is a name to fit, 'Roisin', our rose covered home."

Chapter 4 - 1842 – Roisin, First Balmain House

March the first was a great day, the first day of autumn, after a long hot summer. It was the day Hannah and Archibald packed up their belongings into two of Tom McVey's timber harbour boats. With a willing crew of oarsman from the engineering works they set out to row across to Balmain jetty. Archibald went to grab an oar. John Buller, his best mate, pushed him aside. "No you don't. Mostly you work twice as hard as all of us. Today you ride as a gentleman, in style, with your family."

Their arrival had a holiday feel. They all sweated as they lugged their possessions up the path, to the crest of the hill where the house sat, nestled in a flat space amongst sandstone boulders and a few knurled trees. First up Archibald nailed the metal name plate, Roisin, which he and Tom had crafted in the forge, onto the front wall of the house, next to the door. They all cheered and the adults drank a dram of whisky to celebrate this momentous occasion of having a house of their own. Then, under Hannah's direction, they placed their goods into the different rooms.

There was a cleared space in front of the house which looked across the water, a view part hidden by spiky trees. Here Mary and Hannah set up a picnic. They ate cold meat, bread and cakes, along with lemonade for the children and tea for the adults. John Buller's lad, Charles, was of an age with their James. So the two egged each other into mischief and young Archibald tagged along, trying to keep up.

"Well, it's a fine place you have here," said Tom. "I am sure it will be good to you. Mary and I are even thinking of buying a block here ourselves. While we love our house near the yard we don't need to live so close anymore, and your friend, John here, is married with one cheeky rascal and another on the way. So, we thought, he could take over our place and keep an eye on the yard. Perhaps we could buy land a few hundred yards over there, on the other side of the ridge, where we can look out to Goat Island. I love that view straight up the harbour. As the years roll on, I see myself with my pipe, sitting there watching the water sparkle as ships come and go."

Hannah replied, before Archibald could say a word, "We would love that. While you are both off at work Mary and I will be ladies of leisure."

So, while Archibald went to work each day in the yard, Hannah worked to bring order to her new house and the bushland that surrounded it. Before long she established a garden behind the house and built a brush fence to keep out the wallabies, which otherwise ate all her vegetables. It held a mixture of plants; some she knew from Scotland like potatoes, cabbage and turnips, and other plants she had not known before but that other people suggested she grow, tomatoes and cucumbers were two she loved. Already two climbing roses, one each side of the front door, one pink, one yellow, with their stems pointing skywards, emphasised the name, 'Roisin'. Each morning she admired them while polishing the name plate.

Hannah found this new land strange and foreign, particularly its different animals; the kookaburras still made her jump as they began to call, and she could not help a flash of anxiety at the large goannas and wallabies, though her boys found them fascinating. But she loved the bright light and glimpsed views of water through the trees.

One morning, as she worked in the garden, she saw a tall bearded man slowly walking up the path that passed alongside her house. His head was down and he appeared to be making detailed observation of the plants and rocks. They both happened to look up together. As was her friendly way, she hailed him. "Good day, you look like you are seeking something hidden in the long grass."

"Seeking to discover all of nature's secrets in this strange land," he replied, with a heavily accented voice, *German sounding*, she thought. He introduced himself; "Mr Ludwig Leichhardt, at your disposal, madam."

She found herself smiling at his formal, slightly shy manner. He asked her what she was planting in the garden. Then he told her he was just arrived for a month and still finding his way around. "You would not happen to have seen any aboriginals nearby? I am trying to find out about their customs"

She told him Tom's words about them having abandoned this area. She said she thought there was a camp of them at the head of the bay.

For a few minutes they talked about life in Sydney as fellow new arrivals. He told her of his study and knowledge of the sciences across Europe and his desire to explore the interior of this vast continent.

She told him of her hopes for her family, the boys she had and the child soon to be born, and of her husband's work in the shipyard.

He said he missed his family in Germany but was unable to return.

Soon he went on his way, absorbed again in all the detail of the strange and unfamiliar life of the place. Later in the day he passed again, thanking her for her direction and showing her an exquisite timber bowl that he had acquired from the aboriginal camp, traded for a knife. It was oval shaped, hollowed out from a single piece of timber, the size of Archibald's hand, with ochre markings and etched patterns of animals on the outer rim. He insisted that she keep it, in thanks for her helpful advice.

Years later when he was famous and had achieved his dream, now feted as a great explorer, she would tell of its story and how it had come to her. It always sat in pride of place on the mantel, filled with rose blossoms, or other flowers when in bloom.

It was late June, mid-morning, when Hannah felt her contractions begin. She knew from before that her the baby was coming. Mary and Tom had just moved into their much larger house across the way, so she walked across to Mary's house holding her belly.

Mary hitched the horse to a sulky and they drove to the infirmary, up where the new town centre was being built.

Soon a baby girl was delivered, *much easier this time than the last*, thought Hannah, remembering how long it had taken with her twins in Scotland. Remembering how her mother had been with her and helped at the last birth she decided this child would be named for her. She looked at the soft down on her baby's head and all the past was forgotten.

In the late afternoon, as the light was fading, Mary met the two men at the timber wharf as their boat rowed in. "Well, look at the two of you, a fine pair you are, covered in soot and grime and all the stink of a day's work. You need to get cleaned up, Arch, because you're now the proud father of a new bairn, a little girl.

"Your wife said she is to be called Alison, after her mother. Mother and baby are fine. When you have washed off that muck from your day in the yards I will bring you up to see her. Come to our place as I have hot water for a scrub and clean clothes for you."

Archibald's heart skipped a beat, he knew the birth was near due but he thought there would be another week or two to go yet. Still he was glad that Mary had been there, in place of his or Hannah's mother, and all seemed to have gone well, thanks be to God.

As he walked in to the infirmary room, two small boys holding his hands, he gulped. "You look so beautiful and radiant" he said to Hannah. He turned to the babe. "And who's this wee mite? Alison I hear is to be your name, tis a beautiful name for a beautiful bairn. Boys, say hello to your little sister."

He lifted them up so they all sat on the bed alongside Hannah and the two boys gently touched the tiny hands and face of the baby. Alison opened her eyes and gave a vacant watery look, with just the hint of a smile, before turning her head back into her mother's breast.

Hannah felt the goodness of the moment flow over her, the daughter she had wanted, making her family complete, a continuance passed on from her own mother and grandmother.

Chapter 5 - Hannah

With a new baby and house Hannah soon settled into life in Balmain.

The McVey house was being extended. The first rooms had been built from timber brought across from the yard. Now, a team of masons worked cutting sandstone to build a new wing, which faced north into the winter's sun. From the front of the house the slope fell away, down a rock covered hill, to the harbour. A few hundred yards away was Goat Island, with a view past it, way up the harbour, looking beyond Port Jackson towards the ocean.

On sunny winter mornings Hannah and Mary would sit there, in the shelter of the house, and gaze out quietly, soaking up the view, while baby Alison sat on Hannah's knee and gurgled. Mary had a house keeper who kept the boys entertained in the kitchen with treats and games. As time went by Hannah returned to her dressmaking. Soon she had made four dresses from material Mary had given her. She gave the first one to Mary as a present.

This brought tears to Mary's eyes. "It is so beautifully made. It flatters me so well and that delicate lacework is a perfect finishing touch. I feel you are the daughter I always wanted but never had."

Hannah gave Mary a hug. "You feel like the mother I left behind in Scotland too. You and Tom have been so kind."

They sat in comfortable silence for a few minutes.

Mary suddenly jumped up and left the room, returning a little later with a small wrapped package. She handed it to Hannah. "This is a special thing I want you to have. My grandmother gave it to me as a wee girl. I hoped one day to have a daughter to pass it to. You are the daughter."

Hannah opened the package. Inside, wrapped in a silk handkerchief, was a tiny pale blue-green glass perfume bottle, encased in delicate silver filigree, into which a small blue stone was mounted and with a silver screw-on top. Tears came to Hannah's eyes. "It is so beautiful, I will treasure it forever. One day it will belong to little Alison." She held it out to her daughter to touch.

Alison grabbed for it. With the bottle grasped tightly in her small fingers she turned to them both, showing a bold smile, as if say, "Yours, now mine!" Carefully Hannah removed the bottle from her grasp.

As she held the bottle, resting in the palm of her hand, looking like a sea-coloured, silver encrusted jewel, she felt a huge, unexplained warmth and happiness wash over her. *It is because my life is so good*, she thought. But holding this small bottle made it all so alive and precious. She saw Mary watching her curiously and knew the perfume bottle was indeed special.

Then Mary told her its story, of passing it down through generations untold of her family, each bequeathing joys along the way, so now it was like a treasure chest of happy memories.

Hannah tried to give Mary the other dresses she had made, perhaps as gifts for her housekeeper or friends, but Mary would have none of it, saying, "I know what we will do, this Saturday we will go to Balmain village. We will ask the lady in the village shop if she will hang up your dresses there for you, asking a pound for each. If she sells them it will give you money to buy material to make more."

That Saturday, when they went to the village, Mary was wearing her new dress. As they came into the shop Mrs Mills, the shopkeeper, said, "Why Mary, what a beautiful dress! Wherever did you get it?"

Mary, with a smile full across her face, said, "Why, Hannah here made it. See, she has brought three more which she hoped you might sell.

Hannah unwrapped the dresses, taking each from its cloth wrapping.

Mrs Mills held them to the light and admired them, one by one, all made of shimmery silk fabric with a delicate lace edging. "Oh my, these are really something special. Could I try this one on?" she said, indicating to one that looked about her size.

"Well, you're welcome", said Hannah. "I may have to take in the waist a little to have it look its best".

Before Hannah knew what happened all three dresses were sold; one to Mrs Mills and the other two to her two best friends who came visiting her shop five minutes later. Then Hannah found herself taking further orders from others who came into the shop and admired what she had made.

Saturday, two weeks later, she returned with her next batch of dresses. She did fittings in the back room of the Mills shop, marking out the small adjustments, promising to bring back the final results the next Saturday.

This started a steady business for the two ladies. Mary would cut the patterns and tack them together and Hannah would do the fine sewing. Soon they had enough orders to take on a girl to help. On fine summer mornings they would sit outside Mary's house and work away, while they chatted, and Alison crawled around their legs. Alison often preferred to go to Mary instead of Hannah and clearly thought of her as a second mother or grandmother.

Alison now had inch long, brown hair, with the start of a curl, which Mary tied up with a red ribbon. Mary had Tom make a small-wheeled cart for the children to use. The boys pulled each other and Alison around, bumping over the rocks and roaring with mirth. As the days grew hot they moved into the verandah's shade and worked away.

Soon Alison was one year old. For her birthday they declared a family picnic, with Tom and Mary the official grandparents. Presents were given all round and John Buller and Millicent, his wife, rowed over to join them with their two children as well.

By now they had rented a small shop in the new Balmain village to sell their dresses and do fittings. Their business prospered although the hours of work for Hannah and Mary were long.

Life settled into a comfortable, happy routine; long days of hard work for the men, mostly with an easy silence of companionship and competence. They worked side by side; a mixture of dour Scottish hard work combined with laughter and humour at the world and its demands; the shipowner who swore he needed a refit in three days though he had no money to pay, the dark skinned aboriginal man who came to their yard with a spear and a whole dead kangaroo, carried slung over his shoulder.

He offered it to them in return for an axe. "My name Jimmy. You gime this fella haxe, I givum you dis kangaroo for yo dinner."

Instead Tom took a lump of offcut steel. Indicating with his arm he said to Jimmy. "Here I give you a broom to sweep the foundry floor. Then I will make you your own haxe."

He placed the iron in the forge and, when the floor was swept, he called Jimmy over. "Here, you work these bellows, we need to get that iron bright red." Once it was glowing he pulled it out with tongs. With deft hammer blows he shaped the head of an axe, and made a hole for the handle. Then he found a timber handle and drove it in, before plunging it into cold water. He gave the axe to Jimmy saying, "More better you takem that kangaroo home to your family for dinner. They might be hungry."

Over the water, at Balmain, days of work, mixed with deep friendship, continued for Hannah and her children, with Mary.

Sundays were special days. Everyone slept late then ate a Scottish breakfast of thick porridge, with slabs of buttered toast, black and white pudding and sometimes fresh boiled eggs and haggis. Then they all walked to the Presbyterian Church at the top of the hill, commanding the horizon. Archibald Junior rode on his Dad's shoulders while Alison sat on Tom's shoulders or toddled along next to Mary. James walked solemnly alongside his Dad, showing that he, of all the children, was too grown up to be carried.

After church the routine of a combined family dinner at the McVey house continued, now a spacious sandstone house with a paved terrace, the edge of which fell away down a steep rock strewn hillside to the sparkling water of Sydney Harbour. A large heavy timber table sat on the paving, seating a dozen or more in a shaded corner. On Sundays they gathered here, along with other guests, for a roast dinner. The Buller's were regulars too and the children all played together as the adults enjoyed a long lunch.

In the mid-afternoon, as other satiated guests departed, Hannah and Archibald would leave their children playing under the watchful eye of Tom, who, pipe in mouth and gazing across the harbour, would tell the children stories of his sea days. Hannah and Archibald walked together in the fading afternoons for an hour or two, enjoying time alone together.

Their early years of marriage had been hard; the poverty, the death of little John, and leaving behind so many family and friends, far away across the ocean; all had taken a toll on their happiness together. Now, in this new time and space, their bond to one another grew strong again, with rekindled contentment and affection between them.

Often they walked around the point to the east, beyond their own house and sat on the rocky headland. They looked across to Sydney town, with the windmills of Millers Point standing silhouette on the skyline nearest them, taking in the view of new houses being built below the windmills.

Both loved the way the harbour sparkled in the sunlight, particularly on clear winter's days. They took pleasure watching ships and small boats coming and going from the wharves which lined the western edge of the town. They sensed the poignancy of departures back to England and across the wide Pacific to New Zealand and America. They felt for the hopes and fears of the new arrivals to this strange land. Sitting in this place brought them a sense of connection to their own distant families who they wondered if they would ever see again.

However the early, sharp pangs of loss were fading as their own family filled the hollow space and their contentment with one another regrew. Often they sat silent and contemplative with their hands joined, looking together across the water; other times they would sit half facing, gazing intently at one another, sharing the hopes and fears of their new life. As Arch gazed at Hannah with her steady hazel green eyes he felt a great love well up. When she smiled it was as if a sunbeam washed her face. She, in turn, looked at his dark steady features and knew her life was good.

Sometimes a canoe with black skinned occupants came along the near shore, glistening ebony bodies and fishing spears in hand, as they speared fat cod, snapper and other unknown fish. The cries of delight at each successful capture always conveyed a sense of joy. The aborigines they saw at the edges of town mostly seemed people of quiet despair, unable to deal with life's changes; here remained a proud people in charge of their destiny.

Another year passed. Alison was now two and full of chat, talking and singing in a small clear voice. She had a full head of brown curly hair, showing a splash of gold mixed with red flecked highlights, which fell into ringlets that sparkled in the sun.

She was a strange mix of fun and seriousness. Sometimes, in the midst of her play, she would say incredibly deep things, as if seen through other eyes which had lived long before. Archibald and Hannah then felt she was the wise one amongst them, almost the long grown adult, though still their delightful little girl-child, who ragged her brothers with mock-serious antics.

James, now seven, felt very grown up. Sometimes, on Saturdays, he went off with his Dad, both taking an oar on the row boat, and heading over to the yard to help for a half day.

Hannah loved to sing as she worked in the kitchen, fixing dinner, waiting for Archibald's return from work. Archibald Junior would sing with her as he helped do the chores, his high voice blending with hers. It brought a smile and, at times tears, to Archibald's face, as the beauty of them both, working side by side, with their song, entranced his return.

Archibald Junior loved to sit on his Dad's knee after dinner saying "Da, tell me a story from the yards", and he would tell of a new boat in the harbour or of a job he had done. Archibald Junior was most like his Hannah and, when he looked at his son, with his wide serious eyes, so like hers, he felt his heart melt.

As Alison grew she became almost inseparable from Mary. She would pack her lunch on days when Hannah was busy at work and say. "It's time I went and saw my Gran Mary." Off she would go, skipping up the path, brown hair ringlets in pigtails bobbing. Later in the afternoon, when Hannah came across, she would find the two of them together, sometimes sitting and talking like grownups, the three year old and her ruddy faced Gran Mary. Other times they would be found at work together, weeding vegetables in the garden, making dolls clothes, cooking, or perhaps, working together to draw a picture of a ship in the harbour.

On Alison's first day of school she insisted that both Mary and Hannah come with her, one holding each hand. She walked with them up to the school gate and then gave each a kiss and hug before she ran off to join her friends.

As the years rolled on two more babies came to Hannah; first a daughter, Hannah, to bear her own name, a bright sunny child with straight blond hair, like Hannah's own had been as a child, and which contrasted to Alison's brown hair, with gold and red flecks, and ringed in tight curls. As each new child came, so came a greater fullness and depth to Hannah and Archibald's life together; a love multiplied both between them and with each of these new children.

By 1847 the engineering firm had grown too large for the yard at Mace's wharf and plans were made to move to a new yard in Gas Lane, below Millers Point. Even though the business still belonged to Tom, Archibald and John Buller were like his sons and business partners. More and more they ran the business. Tom was happy to work away on the specific jobs he did best, new ship castings and ship repairs. His twenty plus years had built him a huge network among the ship captains who came to Sydney Harbour. Often he was their first port of call, both to catch up on the news and to organise the urgent repairs needed to continue voyages.

It was one day in May, just before they moved to new premises, when Archibald came back to the yard, after having been out on a ship to work out its refit. The other workers were having their lunch, John was not in for the day, and there was no sign of Tom.

Archibald walked around to the back of the forge and saw Tom, lying on his side, looking dazed. He helped Tom to his feet but had to support him.

Tom mumbled, "Got dizzy and lost my balance." Archibald sat Tom in a chair and called a doctor. The doctor announced that Tom had had a turn and needed to go home to bed.

They brought him home to Mary. Over the next month it became clear that Tom's hard working days were over, he could do simple jobs but had lost much of the power of his arms and the fine dexterity that day to day work in the yard required.

So he called his solicitor and gave instructions for a formal partnership be drawn up in which he held only a minority interest. The new firm, Rodgers and Buller, was established to continue the business in Gas Lane, off Kent St North, and just a short row across from Balmain.

Now, when Archibald came home, he would find Tom sitting on his verandah, with his pipe and Alison on his knee, as he told her stories of the ships he could see, their captains and their voyages. Sometimes Hannah and Mary would be there too, but often just his daughter and the old engineer, wrapped in their own world of the harbour, ships and imaginings.

In 1848, when Alison was six, Hannah found herself pregnant with another child. She felt it would be a boy and decided on the name, Alexander, if it proved so. During the pregnancy she found herself very tired, which was added to by the endless demands of her seamstress business which was booming.

Alexander was a big baby.. His birth was hard and took a long time. He had to be turned by the midwife and Hannah bled much more than with her others. She was very pale and weak after the birth and the doctor and midwife were both concerned for her.

However she was happy that Alexander had survived the birth, looked just like his father, with the dark hair and complexion, and soon was thriving. Now, with a cow for milk, he fed well, even if his mother's milk was little.

Chapter 6 - 1849 -Tragedy

Though months had passed after Alexander's birth Hannah was still tired. She had lost a lot of weight and was only slowly putting it back on. Her smile was as bright as ever and her face radiated happiness each time she saw the children or Archibald, but she now had a delicate look, almost like a porcelain doll.

Archibald thought she was as radiantly beautiful as ever and, if he ever noticed anything was not quite right, he did not say so. But sometimes at night he said, "You gave me a terrible scare when our baby was born. For a minute I thought I lost you. I am so happy that you are still here with me." Then they would hold each other very close and enjoy being together.

Mary worried too she saw Hannah's pale face and was determined to feed her up and get her back to her former strength. Gradually the pallid skin bloomed and the hollows in her cheeks filled again. However, as her strength returned, so too did the demands of the dressmaking business. Soon, once more, every minute of each day was taken up as she worked to fill the orders that continued to mount.

In late February a ship came into the harbour, looking weather-beaten after a long hard voyage. They said that a big storm had blown it off course, just after it rounded the Cape of Good Hope. It had barely made Mauritius for emergency repairs.

On board many of the women and children were sick with fever and a bad cough and twenty had died. Mary and Hannah joined other women from the church in caring for them and, over the next two weeks, many recovered.

But as these passengers recovered Hannah began to cough. Over the next week she developed a fever, though she tried to pretend she was fine. One day, working with Mary, as she went to stand up, her legs wobbled.

Mary rushed over to her and put her hand on her forehead. It was burning. She took Hannah to the bedroom and made her lie on the bed. Then she sent the maid for a doctor, and asked the boatman to row over to the yard and summons Archibald and Tom, who was with him. By the time they came, an hour later, Hannah was barely able talk to them and her breathing was ragged.

The doctor came a few minutes later. After one look deep concern was written across his face. He listened with his stethoscope to her lungs and felt the heat of her body. "It is very bad," he said. "She has severe pneumonia. We will do what we can, but it is not good."

Day moved into night as they passed their vigil. Archibald felt so helpless; he could see her slipping away. He held Hannah's hand, watching her face flushed with delirious effort, with a great stone of dread sitting deep inside him. Mary had taken the children away and put them to bed. They were all very upset and worried about their mother, but finally they fell asleep as Mary held them.

As the clock turned over to the new day it was clear there would be no happy recovery, her face had a blue pallor and her breaths were an endless struggle. Archibald tried to pray but the words ran away. All he could do was hold her hand and caress her face as he felt the life force slip away. An hour after midnight she opened her eyes clearly for a minute. "Oh Archibald, my life with you has been so good, I hate to leave you but I know what this is. Please ask Mary to bring the children in. I want to say goodbye."

With all gathered round she held each one for a second and said their name. When it was done her strength failed. She fell back, barely breathing and, in a few minutes, she breathed no more.

Archibald felt a broken sob wrack his body as his children cried with him.

Mary cried too. "O my child, my poor wee child," she said, over and over again, stroking Hannah's hair. "How I miss you."

They buried Hannah in the newly created little cemetery at the bottom of the hill, looking out east up the harbour, the view that Hannah had loved best. A simple sandstone cross was carved to mark the place. Each day over the next month, the family all walked down the hill to put fresh flowers on the grave.

Gradually life moved on. Archibald had much to do with his five children, though Mary was rarely far away. Often James now went with Tom to the yard to help. Little Archibald had become his father's shadow. Alison and the two small ones would spend much of their days with Mary, who had taken over a mother's role to them. Although he found he could say little to Mary he knew she understood and he valued her support.

Many people in Sydney town were sick with the new flu that had come in on the boat. The graveyard, in the city, now had two new lines of graves, to mark the grief of many. Worst were the aboriginal camps where many died. Their wails echoed over the still night water. Since Hannah's death Balmain had been largely spared.

Each day Archibald, now nine, would walk up to the town, to school, with six year old Alison, while Hannah and Alexander stayed over with Mary and her housekeeper. One day, when Archibald and Alison came home from school, they told their father and Mary over supper, "We can't go to school for the next week. A boy in Archie's class got the flu. It was very bad, and they are scared it may spread. So we have all been told to stay away until next week."

Two days later Archie was coughing and his eyes were running. Mary put him to bed. However that night he had a high fever and he coughed and coughed. The doctor was called and for two days it seemed he was improving. But, on the third day, the fever returned and, like Hannah, his breathing became laboured.

Archibald abandoned his work and stayed by his son's side, talking to him and telling him the stories he knew he loved. Late on the afternoon of the fourth day he said to his father. Tell me about my brother John, the one who stayed in Scotland. Archibald told his son the story of the hard winter, with not enough to eat and that flu, like this, but with two babies only one year old. He said. "You both had it and we feared for you both. But you were stronger and got better, he could not. So we buried him on the hillside which looks out across to the loch, on a cold winter's day".

Archie took his father's hand. "Da, he is calling me and telling me not to be afraid, that we will both be together with Mum soon. Please don't be sad but promise me that you will go and visit him and see your Ma and Pa to tell them too."

Archibald could barely see his son through his tears, but he held his son's hand and stroked his hair like he had done with Hannah. An hour later he was gone, to be with his precious Hannah and wee brother John.

They buried him next to Hannah and the following day Archibald booked a passage on the "Sarah", back to England, to fulfil his son's request. He could not take his children for the trip, and they were happiest with Mary and Tom. So, with an aching heart to leave them, he made his plans to sail.

When time came to say goodbye, Archibald had a sudden desire to leave each child with a special memento. For little Hannah he placed her mother Hannah's gold ring in her small hand. "This will be yours one day, to wear on your wedding day. For now we will keep it safe but you will have it when you are grown". Then, as he cuddled Alison on his knee, he gave to her the silver blue perfume bottle that had come to Hannah from Mary. "This is your mother's gift to you, to remember her by. It holds her favourite perfume. It came from your Gran Mary, a gift passed down from her grandmother and others before. It was one of your mother's most treasured things. One day you will pass it on to your daughter or granddaughter to continue the memory."

Alison held it in her hand, and kept holding it until long after her father's ship had sailed out of sight. How beautiful it was, soft green-blue like the ocean with the silver sparkling like light off the water, and a small blue stone like a bright eye, looking inside her. Something in it called to her, pulling her back to her earliest childhood, happy with her mother. She held it against her cheek, drawing a sense of comfort from it. Finally she carefully put it away.

That night she told Mary. "That bottle is something that will always keep our happy memories in it. Every time I open it I smell Mummy, and it makes me sad and happy together. I feel like she has left her happy memories and love for me in there."

Mary said, "I will tell you the story of that perfume bottle, as was told me by my grandmother, back in Scotland. Her name was Mary too. When I was a little girl, about as old as you, I used to love to visit her house in the next village. Sometimes I would stay with her for a holiday.

"One day, when I was sitting with her as she dressed to go out, I saw her pull out that bottle and dab some perfume on. I asked her about the bottle, as it was very beautiful, and much nicer than her other things. She told me it was given to her by her grandmother, because she had thought it beautiful, when she herself was a little girl.

"The story her grandmother told her was about her great-great-great grandmother, a very long time ago, named Katherine. She had worked as a maid to Mary, Queen of Scots, back when she was a young woman and had first come back to Scotland.

"Queen Mary had much beautiful jewellery made for her by a jeweller in Edinburgh. Queen Mary ordered a new necklace with pearls and diamonds. One day the jeweller's apprentice brought it to the castle, to make final the adjustments.

"Young Katherine, then 15, was serving her lady. She was smitten by this young handsome apprentice and started to secretly meet him. After meeting him several times, one day he brought her a beautiful gift, this perfume bottle, covered in the finest delicate silverwork. He told her he had made it in his spare time in the jewellery shop, when the master jeweller was away, using little pieces of silver he had saved. The beautiful sea-blue bottle he had bought in the markets, from a sailor just returned from the Far East, and he had put in the blue stone because it matched the colour of her smiling eyes.

"Soon after this her mistress had to flee from Edinburgh to northern England with her retinue. So Katherine was forced to leave suddenly before she could even say goodbye to the apprentice. She had cried and cried. She never saw him again, but she still remembered him with great fondness, even after she married and had children of her own.

"She always kept the bottle, to keep the memory alive of her first and happy love. Over time she would take it out when anything special happened, to help her remember. So it became a treasure for her to hold her special and happy memories.

"Then when she was very old she gave this perfume bottle to her own grand-daughter telling her to use it to keep her special happy memories in, just as she had done for all these years since it had been given to her. Since then it had been handed from grandmothers to grand-daughters and sometime to daughters to keep the memory alive.

"I gave it to Hannah when you were a baby and I told her the story. She was like a daughter to me and you my first grand-daughter. She said that in time she would pass it to you and that would keep the memory alive.

Perhaps one day you will give it to a grand-daughter of your own, after you have put all your happy memories into it, to add to all the happy memories that I, your mother and many others have put in there. That way we can pass our love and joy down through the years to come."

Before she went to bed that night Alison wrote this special story into the diary that she kept in the locker next to her bed. After this she pulled out the bottle almost every night when she went to bed, to put her happy memories into it. Sometimes she wrote them in her diary too, to help remember them.

Chapter 7 - Return to Balmain

Since Archibald had gone away James no longer went to the yard. He was often seen walking, slowly and disconsolately, around the headland. He was a steady serious lad, but had always been bright and happy before. Clearly he greatly missed his Mum and his younger brother Archie, who had loyally followed him like a puppy. Now without his Dad to share the burden and give direction he was lost. Whenever he saw Mary watching him he would pull himself up, square his shoulders and pretend all was fine. But, once her observation passed, the melancholy returned.

Tom, since Archie's departure, would occasionally visit the yard, but mostly he left this to John Buller and pottered around at home, carrying his own sadness. After a month of thinking on this and James' melancholy, one day Mary said to Tom.

"It is time for you to get that young lad, James, out and active. You were a keen sailor on the lochs when first I met you, and you still live for the ships. Why don't you get an old sail boat and teach the lad how to sail. It will be good for the lad and it will get you out from under my feet. You're well and truly recovered from your turn. It's time for you to be more active."

So, next day, after school, Tom collected James and they rowed across to Sydney town. An hour of haggling with a small boat builder saw them with an 18 foot yacht and a selection of canvass. Leaving the row boat in the yard, they hoisted a sail and caught the late afternoon sea breeze as it swept them up the harbour. Soon the boat was heeled over and James was flushed with the exertion of steering, trimming sails and changing tack.

That night he ate the best dinner since his Dad left. From then on it was a regular thing; after school and at weekends they would head off, sometimes out towards the open ocean at the heads, other times up different creeks and inlets. Soon James was a better sailor than old Tom.

It would be Christmas in two weeks. Tom hung a lantern with coloured glass to decorate the front yard, and Mary had been baking Christmas cakes and treats. The children were excited, but missing their Dad, hoping against hope that he would be home for Christmas.

As the hot December afternoon cooled with the sea-breeze, Tom and James set sail for the heads. Soon they were skimming over waves, flushed and laughing with exuberance. A mile from the heads, a dark shape came into view, a sailing ship coming in after a long voyage. Something seemed familiar. Tom looked hard and let out a shout. "Ahoy James, that be the ship your Da left on, tis the 'Sarah', back from England. Could it be returned so soon?

"Let's sail alongside and hail them. Perhaps they have news of your Dad."

As they came close they saw people standing in the bow, straining for a first look at Sydney. Suddenly James let out a shout. "Dad, Dad."

Tom pulled out his telescope and looked closely. "You're right my lad. It's Arch, it's your father."

Tom steered their boat in close enough to see clearly while James stood in the bow and waved frantically. Suddenly Archibald's face split into a huge grin. "James, my boy, Tom – how I missed you all."

Tom shouted out. "Come aboard, we'll speed you home long before this old lady gets there".

A quick conversation with the captain and next thing Archibald was lowered onto the deck of their yacht. They flew across the water, all sails up, racing home. They all talked at once but James was determined to show his sailing skills, trimming sails here, tightening ropes there.

Archibald looked with pride at James. "What a fine sailor you are."

Rounding Dawes Point it was straight across to Balmain.

Mary often walked to the wharf, bringing Hannah and Alexander and, at times Alison, to meet the boat, looking out for it as it returned in the softness of evening. Today, as she came to the top of the path, all the children walking with her, she spied the familiar sail boat rounding the point. She thought, *It is early and flying, so much canvass up.* She peered intently, her eyes no longer sharp as before.

She said to Alison, "Have a good look dearie, seems they have an extra one on board".

Alison stared hard. "Yes three people." She stared harder, something so familiar, the shape, the movement, the face.

All at once she knew, even though they were little more than dots. It was her Dad, he had come home. "Dad" she screamed pointing to Mary. Her baby brother and sister took up the chant and they raced down to the wharf. It was all they could do to wait until he stepped ashore. They flung themselves, all together, into his arms.

Next day they all went to the ship to collect his luggage and meet his on-board friends and family. Arch had brought out his younger brother William, William's wife Isabella and their baby son, just older than Alexander. He also introduced them to a pretty, smiling lady in the next cabin, Helen. She was wearing a black dress.

Alison, ever curious, said to her. "Why is your dress black?"

Helen sat down next to Alison and put her arms around her. "Just like you my lovely child. Your Mum died a few months ago. I was coming out to Australia to live with my husband, Colin. But half way here he got very sick and he died too. You miss your Mum and I miss my husband. So I wear a black dress to show that, behind my bright smile, I have a sad place."

Alison took her hand. "I don't want you to be sad. Perhaps we will both try not to be sad together."

Helen looked at this little girl of seven years, with her sheen of bronze-copper coloured hair, and sad, steady eyes. There was something about her, such a wise soul, as if she had lived for a hundred years and seen the worst of what life had to offer. And here she was, offering her comfort.

Soon Helen was a regular guest at their little Balmain House. A month later, one day, Archibald and Helen gathered all the children and sat down with them at the kitchen table.

Archibald said to them, "Helen and I have decided to get married, we wanted to tell you all first".

Hannah, a bouncing three year old gave a bright smile and said. "I want you to be our new Mummy."

Alison gave a shy smile and put one arm through her new Mum's and one through her Dad's arm. She was glad for her Dad that he could be happy again, even though the hole from her real Mum would never go away.

The only ones less sure were Tom and Mary. It was not that they did not like Helen; she was kind and good for Archibald. It was just they still missed and grieved for Hannah, with her daughter like closeness; and the children had become so much part of their family that they hated any idea of seeing them less.

However life continued on, they still saw the children often. Helen was always polite and friendly, it was just that the spark of their love for Hannah was missing. Two things remained constant, Alison and her love for Tom and especially Mary, and James, as Tom's sailing companion.

Alison had found a new friend, a small dark scrap of a girl, whose aunt lived in the aboriginal camp near Blackwattle Bay. She called herself Ruthie, and was about Alison's age but smaller and skinny. Alison met her scouring the rock pools around the point, gathering shellfish to take home. Soon they arranged a regular afternoon rendezvous. Together they explored all the little bays and hillsides, discovering rock caves and treasures, places where only small people like themselves could go.

Twice Ruthie brought her to meet her family. The first time began when Ruthie and Alison were collecting shellfish and other things on the rocky shores at the place where the point of Balmain came closest to the island that her father called Goat Island.

As they traipsed along the shore, scanning for things the tide had brought ashore, they heard a voice hail them in an unfamiliar tongue. Ruthie jumped up from where she was squatting and waved frantically, calling out a stream of unknown words. A man, paddling a light bark canoe, a thing that Ruthie called a 'nawi', came up to them. He carried a short spear with two barbs, Ruthie called it a 'duwal'. In the bottom of the canoe lay four large shiny fish, one still with the spear barbs embedded.

Ruthie explained that this man was her uncle, her aunt's younger brother, and he had speared these fish off the point of the island, a place he called Memel. He was offering to bring her back to their gunyah or camp to share in the meal.

After some more unknown talking Ruthie indicated that Alison and she should both go with the man in the canoe, to share this meal of fresh fish, cooked in the fire coals. So the man lifted them both in and showed them how to balance as he skilfully paddled along, close to shore, until they came to where Ruthie lived. There she met Ruthie's clan as they all sat around the fire in a circle, sharing mouthfuls of delicious succulent white fish flesh.

Ruthie told Alison how her mother, father, two sisters and a brother, along with her father's brother and two cousins had all died in the bad flu that had come before, when the white people died too. Now she lived with her aunty, her aunt's own child, this uncle and her grandfather, a grey haired man called Jimmy. Of more than 30 people who had lived here when Ruthie was little now more than half were gone and her aunt, grandfather, uncle and cousin were all that remained of her own family. She could feel the warmth that this family had for Ruthie, but also the pain of such a loss, even greater than her own. She told them how her mother and brother had died too, and she knew they understood and grieved like her.

After that day it was like they were sisters, two little scraps of humanity who shared their world of memory, pain and understanding.

Alison came once more to visit them. It was a special celebration to which she was invited, by the old man, or so Ruthie said. Old Jimmy had speared a kangaroo and there was food enough for a feast for all. As she and Ruthie sat side by side on the ground, eating the roast meat, Jimmy came to sit with Ruthie, his clear favourite. He showed them an old rusted axe and told them how a strong man named Tom McBee, who worked in a ship yard made it for him, and how it was red like the fire, with sparks everywhere, as he made it. Now, after his best kangaroo spear, it was his most valued possession.

Alison was delighted and told Jimmy how Tom lived close to her and was like her own grandfather, the same as Jimmy was with Ruthie.

Jimmy said, "Ruthie tell me she see that Tom McBee, he live near you in big rock house. You tell this to Tom McBee, he good man and I remember dis haxe he make. Maybe one day I bring him nother kangaroo and we have big feast together."

That night Alison told the story to Tom and her Dad. They roared laughing, till tears ran down their faces, as they remembered. Her Dad told her about the kangaroo Jimmy brought that day and how Jimmy wanted to give it to Tom in return for the axe, but Tom had told him to eat it with his family, as they needed the food more.

Alison was touched Tom's kindness but made them both promise not to tell any others who might laugh at her new friends. After this she told Mary and her housekeeper about Ruthie and they would give her small parcels of food; cakes, biscuits, or sometime a piece of bread and cold meat, for their secret picnics. However, to all the others that lived around there, she said nothing. It was Ruthie's and her secret, just for them. So many other people seemed unkind to the aborigines, calling them dirty blacks, and cursing them. The thought of someone saying this to little Ruthie filled her with a mixture of shame and rage.

One day, as she and Ruthie explored together, they discovered a small tunnel which led to a cave, around on Ballast Point. It was a place where the ships gathered large loose rocks along the shoreline for ballast. Only she and Ruthie knew the cave was there, the entrance was hidden behind bushes and so narrow that only a child or small adult could enter it. A sandstone slab, supported by some crumbling rock, was the roof and there was a dry sandy floor, just wide enough for them to both lie stretched out, side by side. To one side was a small crack, leading up through the rocks, which let in just enough light to see.

This became their own special place, a place Ruthie called Ganing, where they stored their discovered treasures, a piece of rope, a small timber chest, a brass bell, a knife and two coloured glass bottles. Here they would meet to dream, plan and imagine new adventures together.

One day Alison brought Ruthie to her own house, in the mid-afternoon, looking to collect some cake and other treats for a picnic in the cave. No one was home so she brought Ruthie inside with her. While Alison gathered the food Ruthie looked at the things they had. All at once Ruthie gave a little cry. She was holding a wooden bowl, a thing of ochre colours and strange patterns. Alison remembered Hannah saying it was a gift from the great and famous Mr Leichhardt, however since Hannah's passing it had been left to gather dust in a corner.

Now Ruthie was pointing excitedly to the patterns, saying this pattern was one of her clan's totems and that it must have been made by her father or his brother, both now dead.

So Alison picked it up and placed it in Ruthie's hands, saying, "Take it, it is yours now, show it to Jimmy, perhaps he will remember it from before."

Next day Ruthie brought it back, saying Jimmy had told her that it was made by her own father. It was Ruthie's only possession from him. That day Ruthie brought it with her and placed it in the cave alongside their other treasures, tears trickling down her cheeks as she remembered her father. After that, each time they came, she would hold this bowl as her own special treasure. It seemed to Alison that this thing was like her own perfume bottle, a memory keeper for Ruthie to keep her family memories alive.

One night, as Alison was placing her own happy memories in her perfume bottle, and writing some of them in her diary, she wrote in the story of Ruthie's special treasure, feeling it belonged there too.

Archibald resumed his role in the business with John Buller and the business continued to prosper. But, in a way that he could not understand, the Sydney work and his life had lost something from the way it was before. He felt restlessness for something new.

Perhaps it was that, as yet, he and Helen had no children together. They thought children would come quickly once they were married, but now more than two years had passed and nothing. Their life was good together and Helen had taken the place of mother to his children. But sometimes, deep in the night, he would dream of Hannah and feel an ache for her smile. At odd times, when he looked at Alison and saw Hannah's eyes looking back, it gave him a jolt, as if Hannah was still there.

Now his brother William and Isabella had a second child, and he loved this new niece and felt a pang that he could not see her grow. William had worked with him in the yard for a short time and, at first, he and Isabella had shared their small house, until they found a place of their own.

However, after a few months, William headed up the coast seeking new opportunities. He found a job in Maitland, the new port for the Hunter River and a good route to the inland, much easier than crossing those sandstone mountains behind Sydney. Maitland kept growing, surrounded by the good farmlands of the Hunter valley.

William kept encouraging Archibald to come, visit them and see this place. Maitland was now the second largest town in the colonies with more than 7000 people. At the end of the navigable part of the Hunter River, it was the major port to supply settlers moving inland, over the mountains.

In 1853, after three years of marriage, Helen discovered she was pregnant. She first knew just after Easter but said nothing, to stop raising Archibald's hopes. She knew that, for them both, a new child would move their own lives on. As the cold winter winds came sweeping up the harbour, she could feel it begin to show.

One day Mary came visiting Helen and said, "Let us walk together." Mary led her down past the cemetery to the wharf, stopping to place two roses on Hannah and young Archie's graves as she passed, with just a trace of a tear in her eye.

Coming to the wharf she pulled Helen to sit alongside her on the rough timber jetty. She said, "I know there is new life coming to you. While I cannot see it yet I have felt it for more than a month now. It is good for you and Archibald to have your own new child. It will help leave Hannah and the past behind when he holds your new baby. It will also bring much joy to James, Alison, Hannah and Alex to have a new life in the house.

"So it is time for us to become true friends. Nothing can replace my love for Hannah. She was truly the daughter I never had. But, for you and I, that should not come between us. It is in the past. The future is for you and your family. This is something we both care about, so let us become like sisters, or an aunt and niece."

So a new friendship was begun, and Helen found that Mary's wisdom and Tom's gruff humour brought a solid place to her life.

For Archibald too, this new bond of extended family gave him more contentment. Coming home, on warm spring and summer afternoons, he loved to watch Helen's swelling belly as she worked around the house. Then, in the evenings, they would all sit together. As Helen stretched out, resting her legs, she would tell them each time the baby moved, and they would all come over to feel it move too. Hannah and Alex were particularly thrilled about the idea of a new brother or sister and even Alison and James were caught up in the excitement.

Sunday afternoons now became family picnics, often with Tom and James loading the sailing boat and others taking a row boat, and crossing to Goat Island or one of the northern harbour headlands. The adults would laze on white sandy beaches, or under the large shady fig trees which grew near the water's edge, while the children swam in the rock pools or in the shallow waters of sheltered inlets, safe from sharks. Helen would sit with her feet in the cool water to ease their swelling, watching fondly over all her family. Sometimes she and Mary would talk together with a mixture of seriousness and humour about each child; their unrealised potential, funny antics, growing abilities and little weaknesses. Other times Mary would make concoctions and infusions to settle Helen's nausea, ease her back ache or reduce swelling; using knowledge passed from her old Scottish aunts.

Just before Christmas the baby came, Margaret, they called her, small and not so strong, but otherwise seeming fine. All the children were so happy and begged to hold their tiny sister. They endlessly told her how beautiful she was, with her dark eyes.

Then, just two weeks later, it all went wrong. It started like a gripe, with baby Margaret having a pain, then she cried and cried and would not suck and, almost before they had time to realise, she was cold and weak and then it was over. So another tiny coffin was laid in a small grave next to the other two; Margaret Rodgers, born December 23rd 1953, died January 10th, 1854.

A profound melancholy settled over the family. The much wanted and loved child had come, but the visit was too short. Now new life was gone; left behind there was only an empty hole in the family. For Archibald and Helen their shared loss brought them together, but at the same time it left them restless and dissatisfied with life in Balmain.

In February another letter came from William, expressing condolences from himself and Isabella and encouraging them to come and visit soon. They had moved to Newcastle, at the Hunter mouth, and business opportunities abounded. William told of its beautiful coastal location and seaside beaches. He wanted them to come, visit, and see this new town.

Finally, in late summer of 1854, Archibald and Helen caught a coastal steamship to Newcastle. Walking around the flat docklands Archibald felt strangely at home, perhaps it was the name. As a lad he had worked at its namesake in England's north and gained a taste for the world of ships. For Helen, who had grown close to Isabella on the trip to Australia, she found her renewed presence and friendship was wonderful.

As the week passed, before the ship returned, Archibald started to look for business opportunities. Coal was to be had in plenty; all around the town were outcrops of it, and many pits were being dug to mine it. As well the volume of shipping for freight inland was starting to rival Sydney and ship re-fitters and repairers were few. These few constantly needed to send repairs and bring tools or parts from Sydney, a slow, unproductive business with many delays.

One day a local business man, William Trindall, came to him and William with a proposition. "I have a haulage business in Maitland which hauls to the inland. However, I see this new town, Newcastle, is booming. It will soon take over from Maitland as the main Hunter town, because the shallow water of the river to get up there limits the big boats. With the new railway just built between the two towns, I can unload here instead of there.

"I have a piece of land next to town where my haulage business holds unloaded goods. Because ship's captains know me I am often asked to help with repairing ships and bringing goods for ship servicing. But ships is not what I knows and coming down river to Newcastle takes me away from my work inland. I am a bullocky who knows how to haul across the dry miles. I need ships to bring me the goods, but fixing them is not my skill.

"So I need a business partner to run shore operations, receive the goods, store them, send them on to me and fix ships that come to port. My proposal is to give you half this land, on a peppercorn rent, if you become my shore agent. William tells me fixing ships and steelwork is what you are good at. So I propose William here runs my storage yard and you run the ship business. I will look after my teams and their haulage up the valley and to the inland."

Soon it was agreed; Rodgers Iron Foundry and Shipwrights would be established on one half of the site. The other half would become a storage yard with sheds for holding the goods in transit. Before they returned to Sydney the deal was sealed on a handshake. Archibald agreed to return to start work on building their new premises inside the month.

Back in Sydney Hannah and Alexander thought the move to Newcastle was an adventure and James, who had become very attached to Helen, saw the promise of the new business. But Alison was dismayed. She loved their simple Balmain cottage and the stone house of her grandparents was just across the way. Most of all she did not want to leave these dear people, Tom and Mary. They had provided a rock of security and love all her remembered life. And the idea of saying goodbye to her little black friend, her best friend, Ruthie, was too terrible to think about.

But her Dad was firm. She, his oldest daughter, must come and help with their new life. Finally it was agreed, she would come, but each summer she would return to holiday with Gran Mary and Tom, and in the winter they in turn would come to visit in Newcastle and stay for a month or so.

A few days later the move was made. Archibald could not bring himself to sell the little Balmain cottage, Roisin; it held too many memories. So it was placed in the care of Tom and Mary to use as they saw fit. The family's goods were loaded on the boat and soon only the empty house remained.

On the last day Alison took her diary from her bedside locker and found a piece of oilskin and an old tin. Carefully, she wrapped her diary in the oilskin and placed it in the tin. Then she took the tin and placed it into a gap in the rocks, at the edge of the hillside, just behind their house, where the boulders fell away towards the Sydney shore. She placed a loose rock into the hole, in front of the tin, to hide it. Here it would be safe and dry. Perhaps, she would collect it again one day.

Chapter 8 - 1854 - A new life in Newcastle

It was in the middle of 1854 when they moved to Newcastle. Archibald founded his engineering works, 'Iron and Brass Foundry and General Iron Works', at Honeysuckle Point, in lower Church St. They soon settled in and before long the business was booming.

The family's life rolled along and, over the next five years, Archibald and Helen had three more daughters; Helen, Agnes and Anne.

Archibald life grew increasingly busy. He was active as a business man in the city with many interests. He assisted in the formation of the Newcastle Gas Company and was an alderman of Newcastle Council and an elder at the Presbyterian Church which has family attended each Sunday.

He and Helen were happy together with all their children. Alison, their oldest daughter, now had four mischievous younger sisters to contend with. All wanted to do things with her and seek her advice on their clothes, finery and the boys they liked. Hannah looked like her mother with straw gold coloured hair and the fair complexion, but her eyes were light blue whereas her mother's eyes had been dark hazel-green, almost the same colour as Alison's and those of her dead brother Archibald, as her Da and Mary had told her when she was little.

Of her three small half-sisters, children of Helen, the oldest, also named Helen, was good with her books and lessons. The other two were not much interested in learning, but full of mischief with a love for play and dressing up in fine clothes. Sometimes all five girls would sit in the drawing room by themselves, laugh, giggle and tell each other funny stories. If someone came to disturb them they would band together to shoo the intruder away, this was girl time together. Mostly these were happy times, but Alison often felt different from the rest of her sisters. It seemed her childhood, with so many memories, had been left behind in Balmain.

The family shared a love of music, coming from Hannah with her singing. Early in their Balmain life Hannah and Archibald bought a piano, which the family had sat around while Hannah played and sang. Helen, while not such a singer, was an accomplished pianist and continued this ritual. She arranged piano lessons for all the children and music remained at the centre of family activities, sometimes with shared songs, at other times impromptu piano recitals where each child would play a favourite piece, to the applause of others. Archibald, not a pianist, was at times persuaded to play a piece on the bagpipes, tunes passed to him from his uncle in Scotland.

Sundays, with church attendance, followed by an expansive lunch were at the centre of family life. William, Isabella and their children were almost an invariable part of these. Visitors, guests from around the town and foundry workers also often shared these meals and the good company.

Alison and her stepmother, Helen, were close friends. But it was more a friendship of sisters than that of a mother and daughter, having begun with their first shared confidence; this serious little girl who had grown up too young, with the loss of her own mother. Helen felt this lonely hole inside Alison that she was unable to fill She knew that, instead, in part, Gran Mary had taken over this mother's role.

Alison gradually forgot her life in Balmain. For the first six years she visited the McVey's Balmain house each summer and in the winter Tom and Mary came and stayed in Newcastle. But gradually these visits fell away and, as she settled into Newcastle life, her memories of that life faded. She was busy in a house with five younger brothers and sisters to be cared for. As time went by she also started to do the bookwork in the business.

She was now a beautiful, petite woman, already past 21, with ringlets of long brown hair which flashed with highlights of gold and red. Most of her school friends were married with children of their own. But she remained aloof. She seemed to take simple but complete pleasure teaching her brother and sisters and caring for her Da.

Men from the foundry often came around, hoping to gain her attention. While she was always polite her lack of interest was soon clear. Her one true love was for small beautiful things, small trinkets, coloured seashells and stones, miniature paintings, oddments of jewellery.

She collected them from ships that came to port and local merchants. As time went by she began to buy and sell these items, only to people she liked, and always at a good profit. People found that, when they needed something for that special, beautiful gift, then, perhaps, Alison could help. It was her way to give and receive joy and helped fill an empty space.

James was increasingly taking over parts of the business. He had his father's build, tough stamina and also a sharp business brain, which people said came as much from Hannah. While Alison and James were not as close as the others, both had about them a sort of steady reliability. What Alison most liked about James was the way he had taken Helen as his own mother and made her feel a full part of their first family.

James still found time to sail. When Tom occasionally came to town the two would go off sailing for an afternoon, heading out amongst the islands and around the Hunter mouth.

Alexander was the image of his father and, if Alison was truthful, she could not help favouring him. He had the ready smile and charm, with his dark brown hair and eyes. And he could make her laugh. He would dress in finery, like a peacock, and mock himself at the same time. Around the dinner table he would regale them with tales of exploits which would have them all doubled up in laughter.

Yet he had softness too, particularly for Alison. He towered over her, but knew instantly when she was a bit down. Then he would rag her to make her smile. At other times he would turn up with two horses saddled and lead her out on a wild exhilarating ride over the sandy heath covered headlands, rides that left them both laughing and flushed with an untamed zest for life.

Her Da was still himself; now grey around the temples, but with that mixture of strength and leanness of a man at the height of his powers.

Just sometimes he would say to her. "Oh Alison, my special child; you grew up too young. You should find yourself a man. God knows, there are plenty who would burst to carry you away. But there you sit, with wide sad eyes, so like those of my first Hannah. Sometimes my heart aches to make you really smile."

She would go over to him and put her arms around him. "No Da, I am happy, I like being here with you, tis all I want and need."

Chapter 9 - 1870 - Tragedy again

An extract of the Newcastle Chronicle of June 1870 reported:

'The death of Mr Archibald Rodgers took place on Saturday evening 11th June. On 3rd of that month Mr Rodgers, while superintending the lowering of a ponderous iron cylinder in the foundry yard, the palm of his left hand was accidentally crushed between the descending cylinder and another cylinder that lay on the ground close by. Although all was done that medical skill could devise to save the limb, it was found on Wednesday morning that mortification had set in to such an extent as to necessitate the hand being amputated at the wrist. This operation was successfully performed on Thursday by Dr's Bowker, Dagner and Hector. On the following day, symptoms of tetanus appeared, and on Saturday Mr Rodger's medical attendant perceived a change in the worse in him and, at once, apprehended that in all probability he would not live unless a change for the better took place. On Saturday his suffering increased considerably, and articulation became painfully difficult. His consciousness was not much affected till evening when he became slightly delirious and at intervals seemed not to know those around him. He recovered consciousness about 2 hours before he expired and appeared to have recognised some of his family. A few hours prior to his death, the Rev Mr Bain read him the 34th Psalm and engaged in prayer for him. Mr Rodgers was born in the village of Barnyards, parish of Kilconquatar, Fife Shire, Scotland in the year 1814 and was slightly over 56 years of age when he died. His father was an elder in the Original Succession Presbyterian Church at Barnyards, and also superintendent of the Sabbath School in connection with the same church. He therefore had the advantage of an early religious education and ever since he was 10 years old he took delight in imparting similar instruction to the young.

'On the day he was buried all the flags of shipping in Newcastle Port flew at half mast, as a mark of respect.'

Alison stood at the graveside in Honeysuckle Cemetery and sobbed and sobbed. She felt so bereft. She had barely cried when her Mum had gone, though the pain in her heart was like a knife and, when Archie followed soon after, it had hurt double.

But then she knew she had to be strong for her Da. Now it felt as if her whole life was ripped away. Helen hugged her, Alex and James hugged her, her sisters proffered comfort and she knew of their intended kindness, but all she could feel was the void.

Barely a week ago her Da had joked with her, as he walked over to the yard for the day, to remove the cast from that hateful lump of iron that wounded him, mashed his hand.

Then, the awfulness as they cut away his hand, while they fed him whisky, giving him a piece of wood to bite, to hold inside him the screams.

That final horror as she realised it was all to no avail, and watched his body contort with the spasms, until in the end he could not breathe. She had barely left his side for three days as she tried to will him strength and, when all was of no avail, to ease his pain and give him comfort. Now there was just this mound of earth next to the river.

Suddenly she could not bear this place. All these years she had kept the rage inside, to do what was right, to help people; her brothers, her sisters, Helen, her Dad. And it had all turned to dust. She kicked the earth; she hit the hard rock of the gravestone with her hands till they bled. Then she screamed her rage at a God. How could he give her things to love only to then rip them all away? She hated it all, and she most hated Him, for letting it happen.

All at once she knew what she would do. She would go back, return to her beloved Balmain, where she knew Tom and Mary, now stooped with age, tended her much loved cottage, and she would not come back, not ever. She dried her eyes and walked back to the house, her face set in steel. The wake was going on in the living room but she ignored it. Instead she went to her bedroom, gathered her few most treasured possessions and a change of clothes. She wrote a short note, left it on the kitchen table and walked over to the wharf.

A coastal shipper was taking on a load of wool for Sydney. It would leave on the outgoing tide that afternoon. She knew the captain, an old friend of her father's and of Tom and Mary.

"Miss Alison, I am so sorry about your Dad. Can I help you at all?"

She gave him a brittle smile. "I want passage to Sydney. Can I travel with you, please?"

His face burst into a broad grin. "Why of course you can, time to leave this old town is it? There's a spare cabin forehead."

She pulled out her purse to pay him, but he waved it away. "No girl, I can na take your money. Tis the least I can do, to see you safe home to Tom and Mary."

An hour later they sailed on the outgoing tide.

Chapter 10 - Alison comes home

The following day the ship docked in Sydney. How Tom and Mary knew, she never understood, but there they were, waiting at the dock to meet her, looking suddenly old and frail. Tears pricked her eyes as she hugged them, and they held her. It felt so good to have come home. Never would she leave them again. The next day she moved back into her old house, Roisin. For lunch she sat on her front porch and breathed in the familiar fragrance of gum and garden, smiling as she admired the cascading pink and yellow roses.

She knew Tom and Mary would love to have her stay on with them, but this was to be her new life in Balmain, now all grown up, and she had to do this on her own. Besides, not a day would go by that she did not come to see them both. They understood, the love was there, both ways, and that was all that mattered.

In her mind she knew what she would do. Hannah was a dressmaker and had made beautiful things with her hands. She was not her mother and could not do as she did. But she could gather and sell beautiful things, crafted by others. It would make her happy to give happiness to the givers and receivers of the gifts. That afternoon, after she had settled in, she went and told Tom and Mary about her idea. Whether she could support herself through it they did not know, however it was not really about money and anyway James had given her one thousand pounds from her Dad's estate at the foundry.

Tom and Mary harnessed the sulky and together they drove around Balmain village, looking for the right place for her to set up. Just up from the new Presbyterian Church on the hill they found a small shop, with delicate square glass window frames and a vacant sign on it. Inquiries revealed that the owner had returned to London to care for her mother and had left it in the care of her mother's old friend Mrs Mills, now grey and well over 70, but still clear of mind and speech.

"I don't think she'll be wanting it again dearie, and she would be happy with a small rent as it's empty now. In fact I could write to her. Perhaps she would sell it as I hear she is settled back in London," Mrs Mills said, peering at Alison with rheumy eyes.

"What did you say your name was again?' she said, peering even harder. Her eyes lit up with recognition. "It's you dear child, so long since I saw you last and then just a wee girl. When first I looked at you I did not see her, different hair, and features, but then you smiled at me, just the way Hannah used to, and my heart almost stopped.

'Your mother was a most precious soul, taken too soon. It's as if you have brought her back to me. Of course you shall have the shop; it could go to no other. Mrs Maher, who owns it, bought one of your mother's first dresses. Last time I saw her, before she left, there she was wearing it, the silk shining and the dress just as bright and perfect as the day it was made."

In those first crowded, lonely weeks, there were times when Alison craved solitude, even though she knew that Tom and Mary would have loved to see her. She felt as if her intense work was helping her wounded soul to heal, but still she needed time to contemplate alone and come to her own place of stillness.

Sometimes she would go and walk through the small graveyard and sit on a small wooden bench below it, to stare out across the dappled blue water, looking far out beyond the horizon. She found comfort in thinking that her Da and Mum and her small dead brothers and sister were somewhere out there, together.

One day, as she walked down to this place, she saw a woman, a few years older, sitting on the bench. From behind she could see tresses of long black hair flowing over this woman's shoulders and over a beautiful green blue dress, almost the colour of the sea, with delicate silver lace and brocade. A first she felt a flash of annoyance that another had taken her private place.

Then there came a merging in her mind between the lovely dress and her own lovely perfume bottle. It was as if the two had been made together in the same die and casting.

She felt a warm smile wash over her as the stranger turned and smiled. Before she had time to think she found herself sitting alongside her and telling her how her dress so perfectly matched the little perfume bottle.

With kind eyes the lady said, in a heavily accented voice, "When I am a little girl, in Manilla, my Papa, he had many beautiful things, like as with what you say. Sometime, could you show me please?"

So Alison came again the next day, with the bottle in her pocket, and there was the lady again. She showed her and told her about her sadness and the happy memories of the bottle. The lady told her how she often came and looked out to sea in the hope of seeing her husband as he returned in his ship from across the ocean. After that they often both came and sat together in the evening stillness.

In October Alison was working away in her shop when the small bell at the front door tinkled. In strode a man in his thirties, broad shouldered, with a wolfish smile.

"I heard ye was back in town and yet never came to see me. That first moment I heard I got in the boat and rowed across from the yard. I walked up here as fast as I could. James cabled me to say you were in town."

As he spoke she realised; it was Charles Buller, James' playmate from their childhood. Sometimes Tom had taken him sailing with James when they had lived in Balmain all those years ago. She had last seen Charles when she was nine and he was fourteen, a lifetime ago.

Back then, she thought him incredibly grown up and handsome, in her little girl eyes. Now, no longer a little girl, she felt instantly shy and blushed.

He laughed, "I thought you cute then; now I find you all grown up and so, so beautiful" he said, with a courtly bow. "Then a duckling, now become a swan."

Before she could blush again, he continued. "Actually, I come bearing an invitation. My mother is holding a dinner for friends, to celebrate Dad turning 60 tomorrow. When she heard you had returned she insisted I come straight over and invite you, to represent my Dad's oldest and best friend, who we all miss. You will come, won't you, it is tomorrow night."

So Alison found herself there, escorted on Charles arm. Sitting beside him at the table he kept her amused with anecdotes of people he knew and life in Sydney. His younger brother, Richard, mostly ran the yard, working alongside his Dad. Charles, instead, had taken a sailor's life, wanting to see the world; trips to the Middle East, Africa, Asia, London and New York. It seemed so exotic and exciting.

But, last time he returned to port, a few months ago, he realised that it was good to be home. The restless urge was gone and he found he wanted to be with his Mum and Dad in their older years. He also had five young nieces and nephews from his brother and sister and, each time he came back, it seemed they had grown so much. He knew he wanted to be a part of that life.

As the night continued it was as if someone had drawn an invisible link between them, two people who had lived so much of their life alone; two souls connecting in a way neither could begin to understand. Finally it was just the two of them, talking slowly and quietly together, as the last embers of a fire spluttered in the hearth.

Charles took her hand, "I have never talked this way to anyone before. I don't want to stop seeing you or have you leave me, even for a night."

Alison took his face in her hands. "Nor me, I know your Mum has a bed made for me in the spare room, but I want you to bring me back to my house and stay with me."

So it was, as the first light of dawn was touching the eastern sky far out beyond the harbour; that they rowed across to her house. Holding hands, to savour the moment, they slowly climbed the hill. At the crest they stood together, arms entwined, watching, as the dawn flushed the sky with rosy light. Then she took his hand and brought him to her room. They stood next to her bed, with its quilt pale in the early light.

Delicately he took the ribbon from her hair. As it cascaded over her shoulders she unclipped the catches from her dress, and let it slide to the floor, revealing her milky white body. Then she slid her undergarments to the floor, standing totally naked before him.

He gazed at her, mesmerised, "So beautiful, so, so beautiful. I think I have loved you since you were a nine year old girl who gazed at me with those beautiful sad eyes"

"Hold me", she said, "hold me and hold me and love me and love me and never let me go or leave me. I have lost too many people. I could not bear to lose you too."

So he picked her up and carried her to the bed, where he laid her naked body on the quilt. He loved her with wild joy as the early morning sun rose in a pale blue sky. She cried a little when he first came inside her but she held him even tighter, wrapping herself around him until she felt him explode and pour out into her, their bodies and juices mingled.

All morning they stayed together, bodies joining and un-joining, as waves of passion swept over them. In the late morning they slept, in total satiation, knowing what was begun was all good, and would go on and on.

That afternoon they walked, hand in hand, to see Tom and Mary and told them about their new life together and how they would be guests of honour at their wedding as soon as it could be arranged.

Alison knew she had conceived on that first night. By the time they were married a month later she could feel the changes, her nipples and her body softening as this tiny creature grew within her. Two weeks after the wedding, when she was totally sure, she told Charles. He said, I think I felt it too that morning, something that powerful had to create a new life.

In June the next year a boy baby came. They called him John after her first lost brother and Charles' father. He looked like both her mother and father, and something of both Charles and his parents, a fusion of all that was good in all of them. There was quiet completeness in Alison's soul, replacing old with new life, potential waiting to be realised.

A year later Alison felt her body swell again. She knew with certainty this would be a daughter, a continuation in that cycle that passed from woman to woman across generations. So it was that Heather was born. She was a dark child, with the darkness of Charles' mother, Millicent, and of her own father, clear, strong and determined. This would be one to be reckoned with, one making her own path in the world.

Eight years passed without further children. Both Alison and Charles were content, God's gift to them of them of love and two children was more than enough.

Charles discovered a passion for engineering, but with engines rather than shipbuilding and ironwork. He constructed steam engines to use on farms and in factories and tinkered with many other sorts of motors, but electricity most fascinated him. Motors to drive things, using electricity, following the inventions of Edison and Bell, were his greatest passion.

Charles also continued his sailing, first encouraging Tom to sail with him, then little John, when he could swim and hold the tiller, came with him.

Alison flatly refused to let John go out until he could swim across the channel from the wharf to the rocks, more than 20 yards. As Charles could see the sense of this he coached his son's swimming. By the age of four John could swim like a fish, allowing him to go out. James had also maintained his love for sailing. Now he was a successful Newcastle business man, he was often in Sydney, and would stay with Tom and Mary, and the men would all go sailing together; Tom, the old sea dog, barking the orders while the two big men ran to his directions.

Alison's Balmain shop had become known far and wide. People came, both by boat and carriage, to seek out her treasures. She and Charles were well off and could have easily afforded a large shop or a move to Sydney town that would bring extra custom.

But she said. "I have this shop because I chose it, and it is in Balmain because this is where I want to be. Others can be richer and more famous, but my life is rich and I know when I have enough."

Then, in their tenth year of marriage, Charles finally persuaded her to go with him to New York and London while he looked at the new electric power stations and other electric machines. It was a holiday for the whole family and both children found the long steamship passage across the Pacific and then Atlantic Oceans to be strangely enjoyable.

Time to sit, time to read, time to talk and play games. Alison felt her life slow. The bond with Charles and her children forged new links. When they came to London, they caught the steam train to Edinburgh then found a carriage to take them to the small villages of her parents and grandparents in County Fife. Her aunts, uncles, nieces and nephews all welcomed her.

Her own grandmother, Alison, was now frail and her other grandparents all dead. She sat with her grandmother for a long time, two kindred souls, as they joined hands and built a new link, sharing memories of Hannah, long lost daughter and mother.

Then they both walked to the small graveyard, down the side of the hill. Here Alison stood and gazed at the tiny grave of her long lost brother, and beyond to the still waters of the loch. A feeling of great peace washed over her. It felt like a closing of the loop, the final shreds of pain fell away after all those early hard years. Now there was rest and contentment in her soul.

That night she and Charles loved each other with new passion and tenderness, and she knew they had created another life. She felt a longing to be home.

Three months later they stepped ashore at Balmain on a clear winter's day, with clear sharp light. The water sparkled in the fresh wind. Alison tasted the rich smell of gum and ocean and felt the solid rock hill beneath her feet. Tom and Mary did not know to expect them, and she wanted to surprise them. She shushed the children and Charles and they all quietly climbed the path to the top.

There was their dear little house, roses straggling over it, now with two extra rooms joining the side, a bedroom for Heather and office for Charles. She loved it with all her soul, and it beckoned her to stay awhile, but no time to stop now. Instead they tiptoed up the path to where the old sandstone house of Tom and Mary stood; its bulk solid against the sky. She took the door knocker in her hand and gave it three firm raps. A shuffling of feet in the passage, and a voice called out "Who is it?" She knocked again, did she hear annoyance in the old man's voice as he opened the door.

With a squeal of pure delight she pulled the old man to her and hugged him. And there was Mary, silver white hair but those sharp eyes that missed nothing. "Oh my child, my child," she said, gathering Alison to her. "How we have missed you all, and you, John and Heather, how big you are grown, and Charles, Welcome, welcome, welcome. You should have telegraphed; then we would have something ready to welcome you with."

Suddenly, amongst all this chatter, Mary drew back, looking intently at Alison. "I know you, you have your own special news," she said, gazing directly into Alison's eyes and putting a hand to her belly. "My old bones can feel new life. What a blessing is this. Oh, Charles and Ally, what better gift could you have brought me today."

In the full heat of summer the new baby came. She truly was of Alison, the brown hair and those steady green-hazel eyes, and that wise loving soul. They called her Maria, their gift from God.

Chapter 11 - 1872 -Another house in Balmain

Michael Williams was a coal miner from Wales. He had gone down the pit following his Dad before him, as soon as he was of an age. But times were hard there and the wage for a day's work was little enough. His Dad's wages barely bought food for the table.

For Michael, the idea of him slaving his whole life for a pittance seemed a poor choice. So, five years ago, he had packed his few things and bought a passage to Melbourne with the promise of gold and work and wealth. The gold was hard to find and with it the wealth, but there was work aplenty. Those who had the gold were building grand new houses, and the docks were bursting with ships to be loaded and unloaded. After a year working on the Melbourne Docks he took a passage to Sydney to see what it had to offer. He soon found work on the Balmain docks, no shortage of need for human brawn. But this was little different from the mines, the labour just as hard, but at least not down in a dirty hole underground.

He had a room in a boarding house just behind the docks. After his long shifts, when his friends went to the tavern for a pint, he often found himself walking up the hills of Balmain and around the streets, pondering the need for something better to do with his life.

Some fine houses were being built and he wondered if this building trade was something he could learn. There seemed to be a real skill in it in making something to last, different to the endless, useless occupation of moving heavy things from one place to another.

One day he came past a building site as the builder was packing his tools for the day. The builder, a fit young man only a few years older, called to him. "Hey you, not looking for work are you? My apprentice got sick on me and I need someone to take his place."

So Michael found himself with a new job. It was something he seemed to pick up easily. The work was easier and more interesting than moving bales and bags around the docks. He found he had a fine eye for detail and skill with his hands; smoothing plaster after they attached it to the lath board, shaping of the cornices, fine cutting and carving of joinery.

After a year he was the site foreman, building his own houses for Master Builder, Jim Roberts. By now he even had some money saved. In 1871, there were new blocks of land for sale on a street called Smith St. He knew this because he was building a house for a rich merchant on the edge of the ridge where the street crested a steep hill. As he worked there he looked out, across the harbour to Cockle Bay. Blocks opposite were for sale and, when he added in his next pay, he reckoned he should have just enough to buy one.

The day, when his next wages were paid, he collected his money and carried it to the courthouse where land sales were recorded. He counted it out, pound by pound. Sure enough the money was just enough and the land was his, a fine level block at the top of the hill on Smith St.

In his mind he gave this land, where soon his house would stand, the name 'Ardwyn'. It was the name of the house of the rich owner of the mine back home, who lived on a hill top above the mine where the air was clean and he could look across the valley with its dirty smoke and the poor houses of the workers below, to the clear mountains beyond.

Michael had always remembered this house and the name on the front door from the day when his father had given him the job of taking a note up the hill from the shift boss the mine owner. He was just eleven on that day and the vision of that house on the hill had stayed burned bright in his mind as something to dream of.

Now he walked around his new land. A big gum tree stood in the back yard. He considered cutting it down, but thought, "What's the harm of it, it's been there since long before me and there's room for it still." So the tree stayed. Before long, work on his house had begun. Mostly he built by himself, making it piece by piece, using the surplus from other jobs. Sometimes his workers helped him for a few hours in return for a couple shillings on the side along with a glass or two of ale at the nearby hotel. Other times, on the long summer days, when there was still light after the paid work was done, Jim, now his good mate, would help him and together it went much faster. In return he promised to return the favour when the time came on the plot of land Jim has just bought further down the street.

In the tavern, where he sometimes went after work, was a pretty young lass called Rosie, black hair and dark eyes like coals. He soon found out when she was working so he could be there on those days. She always flashed him a bright smile and as he walked in she would have his drink poured and waiting for him. But, whenever he tried to talk to her, his words got all in a tangle and he would find himself going red and sounding stupid.

One day she was not there and another girl, Margie, who normally worked in the upstairs bar, was in her place. He mustered the courage to ask her if she knew where Rosie had gone.

Margie replied,"Oh, her Ma is sick and she had to stay home and mind her for a couple d ays. So you're Michael, the one that she likes but says is shy. Why don't you ask her out sometime? She lives in Montague St you know, number six."

Michael went bright red, but felt a thrill run through him. He thought, *Could she really like me when I act so stupid in front of her?* He walked out of the bar when his drink was finished and took a deep breath. It was now or never. He called to the flower shop on the corner of Beatty and Montague Streets and bought a bright coloured bunch. Standing in the front of the house with the number, 6, in fancy brass writing on the front door, he though it looked too grand to visit. He could feel his knees knock and hands shake. Finally he managed to bang on the knocker.

Rosie answered with a bright smile and raised eyebrow "Michael?"

He felt his face flush and stumbled out. "I heard your Mum was sick. I brought these for her," as he handed over the flowers.

Rosie went bright red too. Almost at once she burst out laughing. "Oh, I thought these were for me and did not know what to do, I was so excited" Spontaneously she gave him a hug. "Thank you so much, that was such a nice thing to do."

Again he went red. Now they both laughed. "I was really thinking about you when I bought them," he said.

"I know and I like you too. I told Margie at the upstairs bar how nice you were. I hoped you would ask me out or something. Well let's not stand here, you must come and meet my Mum, Sophia, she's from Spain you know. That's where my black hair comes from."

Sophia was sitting in bed when Rosie came in. "Mama, I have brought you a visitor, Michael Williams, and he has brought you flowers"

Sophia's face lit up. "Oh so beautiful, bella, bella."

Then she threw back her head and laughed. "Perhaps these flowers are for you Rosie. Such a handsome young man, who I have never met before, would hardly bring flowers for an old lady like me, when there is a beautiful senorita in the house.

"Well do not leave him standing, a glass of sherry for our guest and another for me"

It was Rosie's turn to blush as she went off to bring refreshments.

After she left Sophia turned to Michael and said, seriously. "It is good sometimes to flatter the mother, no, though your eyes say Rosie, Rosie. She has already told me she sees you in the bar and likes you, before today. So it is good to meet you at last. You be kind to my girl, she has been sad since her father not come back." With this the pact was sealed.

Chapter 12 - Sophia

It emerged that Sophia was from Spain but had lived in the Philippines since a child. Mother and Rosie, together, told him the story of how, in 1851, a young ship's captain, Edward Martin, from Sydney had sailed into Manila harbour seeking a load of teak for building in Sydney, to be supplemented by such finery and silks as he could arrange from the far east. The merchant who provided the lumber was one Senor Carlos Rodriguez.

Senor Rodriguez was a timber merchant who had prospered on trade with Spain and England. He could also supply, through friends and business partners, many of the other goods Captain Martin sought. He was keen to build his business opportunities in the new south land, they called Australia and to which the settlers were now heading in big numbers.

He had heard stories of gold discovery in Australia and, arising from this new wealth, he saw opportunities for his business to grow, timber for houses, food for hungry workers, fine clothes for ladies. All these things he could source locally or from nearby China or Malaya. So he was searching for news about this place, particularly more about the rumoured gold discovery and the prosperity of Sydney.

Young Captain Edward Martin, who had just arrived, having sailed out of Sydney, seemed an ideal source. At first the Captain was cautious, polite but non-committal. So Senor Rodriguez invited him to dinner at his house. He hoped, with wine and hospitality, he would learn all the Captain knew. His wife was indisposed so his seventeen year old daughter, Sophia, took on her role as hostess.

Sophia was impeccably groomed, with a pale green silk dress and her black hair tied back. She had a ready smile and laughed at the Captain's jokes, even when he suspected that that she did not understand. He found her accented English intriguing. His father explained that she had been tutored by an elderly man from England, who had lived in Malaya for a time. From him she had picked up a passable command of English.

By the end of the meal, not only had Captain Martin given to Senor Rodriguez all the information he possessed but the Captain was moonstruck.

For the next few days, as the loading proceeded, he did not see Sophia again but could think of little else. Then,, on the day of his departure, Sophia accompanied her father on board, when all the bills of lading were finalised, before the ship sailed. While all documents were checked off by the first mate and merchant, before the captain too made his final check and signed for their receipt, a brief opportunity came to engage Sophia in a conversation. He sensed that she had also been seeking a chance to convey her interest. As Sophia later admitted she was equally enthralled by this tall young sailor with blue eyes and tousled blond hair, so different from her family's dark looks.

Captain Martin asked if he could see Sophia again should he return. She gave him a shy smile and a small nod of his head. She indicated that her father's permission would be required.

As he weighed anchor and eased off the jetty, both father and daughter waved, and he waved back. Sophia was standing behind her father, out of his line of sight. As she turned to go she touched her fingers to her lips, as if to send a kiss.

Back in Sydney the supplies were well received and he was immediately commissioned for more trips. When next he returned, he went immediately and asked her father's permission to court his delightful daughter. More easily than expected the father agreed. It was a strictly chaperoned affair. It could be, he thought, that Senor Rodriguez saw his daughter as making a business opening for him to the port of Sydney.

At this point, Sophia, who was telling Michael the story, as if through her husband's eyes, laughed. "In fact it was me that helped my father to have this idea. He liked my Edward well enough but did not want him to take me away. It was only when I made my father see the business opportunity in my going to Sydney that he relented. Even then, I had to beg him many times and most earnestly."

Michael found himself strangely pleased with this thought of Rosie's mother's contrivance. It was as if she recognised and gave unstated approval to his own efforts to impress Rosie.

The lady continued. "I also had to encourage Edward so he did not become disheartened with all our courtly manners and slowness. But he genuinely liked my father and also liked his clever business brain, which was like his own. And he knew my father's affection for me was real as was mine for my father. Though I would have married no one else I would not have gone against my father's wishes to marry him."

Rosie continued the telling in the third person. She had heard this story many times, as told to guests at dinner parties by her mother and father. "Senor Rodriguez had other grown children, a son who helped in the business and a daughter married to a Spanish gentleman in a fine house in Manila, but it was Sophia who was his favourite and brought the fondest smile to his face.

"Before his next trip to Manila my father took all the money he could raise to a fine jeweller in Sydney and had him make a fine gold watch for Senor Rodriguez, a delicate silver necklace for his wife and, for his Sophia, a string of pearls.

As soon as he returned to Manila her immediately sought out Senor Rodriguez, gave him the gifts, and asked for his permission to marry his daughter. Senor Rodriguez accepted the gifts and indicated that he would need to time to consider. The next day the Captain was invited to a dinner with the whole family. The father, mother and daughter were all wearing his gifts. After the meal the ladies retired and Senor Rodriguez and his two brothers considered the request. Finally it was agreed, the proviso that they must marry in the Catholic Church and that any children were to be baptised as Catholics.

It was a big family wedding with more than two hundred guests, held in the white walled church in a town at the edge of Manila, where many other grand houses were. They remained with the family for two weeks before they returned to Sydney to live."

Sophia continued. "Almost 20 years have passed since we built this house in Balmain into which Rosie was born. I hoped and hoped for a second child, a son for my husband, but God did not grant this. But we were very happy, and Rosie loved her father dearly. Then, one year ago, when the return of Edward's ship, Adelie, from a voyage was overdue, news came that it had been wrecked in a storm far out in the Southern Ocean. All that was found by another passing ship were a few small pieces of wreckage, just enough to confirm its identity."

Sophia and Rosie held each other's hands while she said this, tears in both sets of eyes. They told how they clung to each other in their grief and, already close, this brought them even closer. Now, without a captain's income, Rosie had taken work, to allow them to keep their fine house in Balmain. It was only since Rosie had seen Michael in the bar that she had begun to smile again.

From this day on Rosie and Michael were rarely apart. Soon they were planning the finishing of their new house in Smith St. It may be small but it must be beautiful, fine fireplaces and high ceilings, and places for pictures. It would be a fusion of Spanish and English styles. Together with Sophia they chose the name 'Casa Ardwyn', house on a hill, to tell of its shared heritage.

Six months later Sophia summonsed her brother, Jose. He came to Australia to stand in for her husband, Edward, to undertake the father's role to escort the bride. The wedding was held at St Augustine's Catholic Church, at the top of the hill in Balmain.

It was a beautiful spring day, their house was finished and Rosie was radiant, with white scented flowers in her hair, as her Uncle Jose led her down the aisle in the church. His own wife had died two years before and it was decided that he should stay on with his sister to provide family for Sophia and the new couple. Rosie's friend, Margie, was bridesmaid and Jim Roberts was Michael's groom. By the end of the night Jim and Margie were shyly holding hands as well.

Next morning, early, Rosie was up and working in the front garden. Michael went out to see what she was doing and found her placing a small plant, just a few inches high, in the soil. He grasped her from behind and pulled her close. "What are you doing?"

She replied, "When I was a small girl, my father took me on the boat one time, with Mama, to her house in the Philippines. It was a happy time and the thing I remember best, which we all loved, was the scent in the air around their house. It was of frangipani, so I asked my Uncle to bring us a plant from their house to here, so it could grow in the garden of our new house. Each time I smell it I will have a happy memory of my father. So, even if he cannot watch our children grow, this is something for them to remember him by.

A year after this their first child, Edward, was born, named after Rosie's father. Then came Robert for Michael's father, Margaret for his mother and Rosie's best friend and finally Jimmy for his best man and friend.

It was a happy house, though, as more children came, it soon seemed too small. They added a back verandah for the boys to sleep on and Margaret had the front room. As they grew up there was often the sound of laughter, as games were played in the living room. Jim and Margie were married the next year and they now had two boys and a house down the hill on the other side of Smith St, so the kids were often in and out of each other's places.

Their building business boomed and they were now full partners, each at times building their own houses and sometimes working together on the big jobs like a new Town Hall, at the corner of Darling and Montague St.

Finally, after eleven years, when Jimmy was six, they all moved into Sophia's house in Montague St, as it had space for them all. They rented their cottage in Smith St for a year. One day Sophia came to them and said. I know there is room for us all here, and I love all the children, but I love the cottage in Smith St with the frangipani in the front yard and its Spanish name. Every time I see and smell it I am reminded of your father. I would like to live there with all those good memories.

So it was agreed, it became Sophia's house. Michael gave it a new coat of paint and built a picket fence and a new fireplace of pink porcelain in the front room for her to sit by, where she could watch the passing life in the street. Jimmy, always her favourite as the youngest, would call to see her almost every day, he loved his beautiful grandmother, Sophia, her hair now silver and those dark flashing eyes, so like his Mum's. Often he would sip a small glass of sherry with her as together they watched the world pass.

As the years went by Jimmy was often in trouble, fights at school and poor attention in classes. It was as if the success of his older brothers and sister made him resentful. He left school early and took work in the docks, and then moved out from home to make his own way in the world. Sometimes he would go weeks without seeing his parents, and often he was dirty with ragged clothes. But Sophia never cared. He was still her favourite grandchild and there was always a place for him in her house. With her he was able to feel loved and clever, not the ne'er do well younger brother.

Finally in her 64th year, 1898 just before it came to a close, Sophia grew suddenly ill and weak. By early the next year she was gone to that place where her own husband awaited her.

They buried her in the small cemetery at the foot of the hill at East Balmain, where she could watch the ships come and go, as she had all those years before with her little Rosie. As Jimmy stood there, alone, after the others left, saying his private goodbye, he saw other headstones also standing silent, sentinels to the view; Hannah Rodgers aged 32, Archibald Rodgers aged 9, Tom and Mary McVey, both in their late eighties, were some he remembered.

Chapter 13 - 1899 - Jimmy William's match

Balmain was abuzz as it came towards the start of the new century, 1900. The town was crowded. The 1890s had been tough. Once a sleepy little village and place of the well to do, Balmain had now become the dormitory suburb for thousands of poor, working class people. Crammed into small tenements, narrow terraces, and dozens of dockside boarding houses, thousands of workers eked out an existence. The grand building boom of the 1870s and 1880s had faded into the depression of the 1890s. Thousands of people flocked here searching for jobs, lining up in long queues in the hope of a day's work, stacking lumber or loading wool bales on the docks.

Jimmy had been mostly happy while Sophia, his grandmother, had been alive in the Smith St cottage. But he was now he was almost 23 and jobs were hard to find. His father and Uncle Jim's building company had fallen on hard times. Perhaps, if he had begged, they would have found him some work, but he did not beg. More days than not there was no work to be had.

Jimmy found himself afflicted with a strange melancholy now that Sophia was no longer there to give him encouragement and wise counsel.

The empty house in Smith St was boarded up to stop squatters, and the garden was weedy and overgrown. Perhaps his Dad would sell it; clearly his business needed the money. But there was little money to buy houses, and anyway he hoped it would not leave the family. This house was special in his heart, early happy memories, and his sanctuary while Sophia had lived.

Still it looked like a dump now, rubbish in the front garden, boards over the windows and big signs proclaiming *Trespassers Prosecuted*. It would break his Gran, Sophia's, heart if she saw it now. He thought his Mum and Dad should care more about it; after all it was first their house, the place they built together. They had even given it the name, Casa Ardwyn, to recognise both their histories.

But his Mum and Dad now lived in their grand house in Montague Street and mixed with the high life. Mr Barton and his Federation mob were all the talk. Mr Parkes, although he was dead now, had also lived in a big house in Balmain, Hampton Villa it was called. His Mum and Dad used to visit there for drinks and parties. Now it was the Barton crowd they visited. It seemed the hard life did not affect those people, even though the way his father talked their building business was barely surviving. But he still seemed to have money for all the political meetings and hobnobbing. It was said that next year the Queen of England would sign a deed giving Australia its own independent government. That was grand and all, but really just a thing for the snobs and high rollers of government. Few of his friends from the docks cared about such rubbish.

For them life was occasional days of backbreaking work and many more days of sitting around doing nothing. Inevitably they all ended up in the pub if one had a wages packet. Often, after a few beers, a fight broke out over some silly thing, whose dog was best, whose football team was best, or perhaps they fought because they were all bored and needed to do some real work, to do something that achieved something. Anything, just anything, except stacking timber, wheat bags and wool bales. God, how he hated those things.

Today he was going to the Exchange Hotel, someone said drinks were half price and there might be a two up game on. That was one thing he was good at; he was fast and knew a few tricks. He could usually make a few bob there; at least enough to buy another drink, that's if someone did not call him for cheating and he ended up in yet another fist-fight first. Already his nose was a bit out of shape, where it had been hit a few times and he had a scar beside his eye and another on his cheek where a couple of left jabs had connected.

Jimmy felt his life was passing him by and he was turning into a wastrel, but he did not see what was to be done about it.

Sure enough, the Exchange was crowded, with a two up game in full swing. He tried to shoulder his way in, close to the action. There was a new girl in the parlour where the genteel folks went for a drink,

Maggie or Marie, maybe Maria, was her name, or something like that. She was a looker, gold-brown curly hair with just a tint of red and a fiery temper when crossed, or when the boys tried to make a pass at her. But she was nice to him. Pity he had no money, beyond the price of a beer, or perhaps he could ask her out.

As he thought of her he found he had made it to the front of the two up circle. He watched the coin toss a couple times. He had a couple of coins like those in his pocket and one was special with extra weight to make it mostly land heads. Perhaps he could slip that one in for a bet. He waited till the coins were flying high, near him. He put his last five shillings on the next bet for heads. As the coins flew high he made out to stumble and, as the coins landed next to his feet, he managed to grab the flying coin and drop his own in its place.

He was sweating but he was ten shillings up and no one had noticed the other coin. Now, soon, he had to get it back before it was spotted. He moved around the circle a bit further to get to where it looked like the next throw was aimed.

But a big Irish bloke blocked his path. "Where the fook do you think you're going. I don't trust you. Yoose one of those smart arse kids who tinks you don't have to play fair and square. I reckon you're running a scam. I've lost a pound since you came. I know you're up to something, little fooker".

Jimmy was quick and tried to duck under the monster's arm. But this bloke was quicker. Before he knew what had happened he had been grabbed by the collar and backhanded. It knocked him sprawling right into the path of the flying coins, so at least in the confusion he got his own coin back.

He hit the dust at the edge of the circle. With the momentum his head smacked into the post holding up the verandah, a great whack across the side of his face. It felt like his cheek and jaw was broken. Stars spun in his eyes and he tasted blood in his mouth.

He heard someone say, "Serve the cheating fooker right." He felt himself pushed out of the way while the game went on. Then he was dragged along the floor and dropped somewhere cool and dark. He lay in a dazed state, with blood trickling from cuts on his lip and below his eye.

He must have passed out because, when he awoke, gentle hands were cleaning his face with a wet cloth. He opened his eyes and winced, *Bjeez his head hurt*. Then he saw her face, like a fiery angel, framed in a haze of golden red hair, lit from behind by light through the window.

"Well, crazy boy they messed up your pretty face proper. I am trying to fix it up but it won't be anyway pretty for the next week or two". Then she did something that seemed totally remarkable. It convinced him he was really dreaming or she was an angel. She gently stroked his forehead then planted a soft kiss right where her hand had been.

Suddenly their eyes met and she went bright red. "I don't know why I did that," she said. "I just felt you needed something kind after what they did to your face. Still, it's really your fault, you silly boy."

She jumped up. "I must go; my Ma will be waiting for me."

Slightly dazed, Jimmy stared at the space where she had just been and breathed in her faint scent, which lingered. He could not let her go like that. So he stumbled to the front door, just in time to see a older lady pull up in a fine carriage and his angel give the lady a flashing smile and climb up.

Before they could drive off he managed to get to the horse's head. He stood up straight and tried to catch her eye. "I am sorry, I never said thank you for helping me. I don't even know your name."

The oldervlady looked at him with a raised brow and a trace of an amused smile. "My name is Alison and my daughter is Maria. Pleased to meet you. Perhaps you will visit my shop, near the church with the steeple, over there, when you are feeling a bit better."

With that she gave a flick of the reins and they were gone. There was something about mother and daughter, not the same but both cast from the same fiery mould, she with her red-brown hair turning to grey, and Maria with the fire in hers. It was those same eyes, dark hazel flecked with green, both knowing and a touch sad, but with such a force of life.

Three days later, when the worst of the purple bruises were gone from his face, and the pain in his head was but a dull ache, Jimmy found his best clothes and scrubbed his body until it felt clean. Then he brushed his hair, polished his shoes and put on his jacket. For once he called to his mother.

Rosie was surprised but happy to see him, particularly clean and tidy.

"Mum" he said. "I need ten bob for a present. I promise to pay you back next shift, but I really need the money today."

"Jimmy, I know something important has happened, even if your face is not its best. Here take this; if it's important enough to get cleaned up it must deserve your very best, something memorable. I don't know who she is but I am glad it has happened." She pressed a gold guinea into his hand.

Jimmy was used to getting his way with the girls, but today he felt nervous. He took his guinea and went to the shop near the corner of Darling and Montague, where they sold brooches. He chose one with an amber stone, with just a trace of red, set in silver, to match the colour of her hair The price was written on the back, £1.10/-, however the lady agreed to take his golden guinea.

Next door was a fancy cake shop. He really felt he needed something for the mother. There, in the corner of the window, was a luscious, strawberry and cream topped cake, decorated with little gold and silver balls and chocolate stars. It seemed right. The price was ten shillings. He felt in his pockets hoping against hope that he might find enough money but all that was there was a few pennies, a sixpence and a couple shillings.

He was about to walk on. Then he remembered something that had almost gone from his mind in the dazed state of three days ago. His ten shilling note, winnings from the two up. He seemed to remember, he had taken it from the pocket of his blood covered shirt, and placed it inside the breast pocket of the jacket in his room, the one he was wearing now. He patted it down, something was there. Sure enough, his ten shilling note had somehow survived, just for this.

In he went. The cake was his, carefully placed into a cardboard box decorated with a silver ribbon. The lady who served him seemed to know how important this was. She even placed a selection of small cakes and toffees as decoration around the outside of the strawberry cake in the box. As he walked out she called after him, "Good luck!"

A few minutes later he found himself outside a small shop near Saint Andrews Church. Brightly painted above the door was 'Alison's Antiques and Special Gifts'.

With his heart pounding he stepped inside. It was only him and the lady. She gave him a warm smile. "I was hoping you would come, I thought it might be today."

She walked around the counter, stood in front of him looking squarely up at him and placed both her hands on his shoulders. Her eyes searched his face with an intense kindness, as if trying to look deeply within to see what goodness was buried there. "You will have to look after yourself better if you are to be the one for my Maria. She needs a one who is steady."

She stepped back and smiled. "Well enough of that. I see you come here bearing gifts."

Looking at all the exquisite things arrayed around her shop Jimmy felt inadequate; it was all so much more and better than his gifts. He took a deep breath and felt his poise return. He stepped forward with confidence and placed the cardboard box on the counter. "I thought you might like this."

She opened the lid. Her mouth opened, making a small gasp of delight. "Strawberries and cream, my favourite; look at those delicate little cakes and toffees. We must each try one at once."

She took a toffee placing it in her mouth with a look of blissful delight. "Please try one too, they are delicious."

So he took one and felt the luscious flavour coat his mouth.

"Oh, but they are sticky," she said.

They both stood, grinning and laughing, like two mischievous school children caught eating candy. "I see we will get along famously," she said.

Then she became serious again, "But I know you did not really come here to see me. I am sorry to say that Maria is not here today, although she often comes in to help me when not working in the Exchange Parlour. But today she had to go in to the city to look at some things for my shop. She will be back at our house about three o'clock this afternoon. Why don't you join us for afternoon tea, this cake would be perfect. My carriage will leave here about that time. I would be pleased if you would accompany me there."

Jimmy wanted to skip and cheer as he walked out of the shop. What a lady Alison was, and he just wanted to see Maria's face as she looked at the brooch, please to God that she would like it. It was now just after eleven in the morning and he had more than three hours to wait. What should he do to pass the time?

Part of him felt a pull to share his excitement with his friends at the pub, and have a beer to calm his nerves. But he knew, deep down, that today was far too important for that. He walked the streets, restlessly at first, then he settled into a methodical pacing. Without intent his steps led him to the old house in Balmain, his grandmother's cottage in Smith St, still the old battered name plate '*Casa Ardwyn*', half fixed to the door.

It was as if cogs were whirring in the back of his brain, now alive to new possibilities. He did not want Maria to see the old girl in this state, already his mind had a picture of them living there together, their children playing on the front verandah, as he and his brother and sister had when he was little, often with Rosie and Sophia sitting on their stools and chatting while they watched on. There were scents of frangipani, wafting on late summer afternoons, as they played under leafy branches, shaded from the hot afternoon sun. Sometimes there was a big fire in the bush behind, just across the water; and little half burnt leaves and twigs would fall from a grey hazy summer sky, down into their garden, and they would hear the noise of the fire engines racing to save lives. But they had always felt safe in their little house.

The daydream had transported him. He looked up again at the sad reality. Half broken fence, piles of rubbish, a broken stump with a few leaves shooting in one place was all that remained of their old frangipani tree.

He took a deep breath, time to get to work. Walking round the corner to the West End Hotel, he asked the barman for an old burlap sack.

The barman replied, "What no beer today Jimmy, and very posh we are with that jacket."

Jimmy could not help grinning, "I have work to do.'

He set to work, gathering the mouldering boards and papers, broken branches, cast off rags and all the other detritus which filled the yard.

He was conscious of not getting his best clothes dirty or smelling like a tramp for his afternoon tea. He stepped back and examined himself. Only a few specks of dirt so far that he could brush off. The burlap bag was already three quarters full.

But the rest would have to wait for tomorrow; he would get to work then in his old clothes. He knew what he would do, tonight he would call to see his Mum and Dad, and ask if he could borrow some tools to fix the house and then start living there. Perhaps they could even lend him a few pounds to buy paint for it; in his mind he pictured the house a soft lemon colour and Maria sitting with him, outside, wearing a sky blue dress.

It was time to go. He suddenly realised that the day had flown. In haste he found his way back to Darling St and the shop, hoping she had waited. The shop was closed and he felt mild panic. He came around the side into the shade. There she was, sitting in her carriage, surveying him with a cool stare; as if assessing whether he had failed his first test.

He just grinned; nothing could spoil his day now. She made space for him to sit alongside her, up front, and headed the horse down Darling St towards East Balmain.

He found himself talking to her, telling her about himself and what he had been doing, his grandmother and how he missed her, the old house and his dreams for it, his rough life and troubles. It all came spilling out. She listened quietly, taking it all in, as if she knew and understood half already.

Finally she said. "My Maria is a bit like you. Her life should have been easy, she was given much. But sometimes that is not enough and you have to find your own way. Sometimes things do not go right. She too has had her troubles, but now she is grown and moving beyond that. She is a good girl but often she wants to fight the world. You and she, I think, could help each other."

So absorbed was Jimmy that he barely noticed the road. With a start he realised where they were, as they pulled up to a stop in East Balmain. It was just above the cobbled street that led down to the ferry, past the graveyard where his dear grandma, Sophia, was buried.

Again he found himself telling this to Alison, and of how Sophia had been placed there to look out towards where her husband's ship would come in, even when it never had.

Alison smiled and looked kindly at him. "This I know. She too was my friend when I first came back to Balmain, and I was the lonely one. She told me the awful news on that day when she found out that her husband's ship was lost, far out to sea. We cried together on that day.

Then I saw you standing there, after all the others had left, when they buried her, and I knew your sadness. My mother, my little brother, my sister and my dearest second grandparents lie next to her. They too loved the view. On that day I could feel your hurt and I felt, perhaps, it was you who would make my Maria happy.

Today, when you did not come back, I feared that you were not strong enough for her and had returned to your drinking. Now I feel I know you better and that you and she will make each other strong.

We will go to our house soon. But first I want you to see another most special house."

She dismounted from the carriage and led him off Darling St down a small lane to the east where the view opened out to Sydney town. Perched on top of the hill was a weatherboard cottage, with a sandstone fence and lots of roses growing in the front garden.

"This now is my daughter, Heather's house, where she lives with her two children. But, once, it was my parent's house and then it was my house. Here I found and knew love, and this house shared it all. It is like the love you feel for the house in which you first lived, and where you hope to live with Maria someday. Now Charles and I live in another house that I love too, but this house will always be most precious for me."

Jimmy felt a surge of affection for the lady who stood beside him; it was as if they had known each other all of his life.

She turned and took his hand in her own small hand and led him back across Darling Street, to where the land fell away to the other side, down another lane. She passed him the reins to lead the horse as they walked side by side. Around a bend in the lane stood a grand sandstone house, its bulk rooted to the earth and its towering sandstone walls holding up the sky. He saw the name 'Ocean View' written on an ornate plate next to the door.

Chapter 14 - Maria

Jimmy looked up at the house in awe. His mother and father lived in a grand house in Montague Street, which perhaps was larger. But this house had a presence which riveted him. It belonged so completely in its landscape, stone rising from stone, honey coloured hues, embedded within its gardens. This house belonged to and completed this land, giving it living continuity.

Through the open front door he could hear a voice singing, it sounded like an Irish folk song. Alison put a finger to her lips. They came along the passage, out into a sun filled room.

She stood, her back to them, small alongside a broad shouldered older man, working side by side on a bench. Sunlight cascaded through her hair, flashes of red and gold. The older man was humming softly but her voice lilted and soared with a pure ethereal beauty.

He and Alison stood transfixed, caught in the joy of the moment. It was like an invisible signal passed between Alison and the man. He straightened, squared his shoulders and slowly turned round. As he saw Alison his face moved from simple contentment, working alongside his daughter, to a full infectious delight as he saw his beloved wife, there, before him. Despite their years love radiated between them like a stream of pure light.

Jimmy saw this but it almost passed him by, so transfixed was he by the glowing hair and song. On her father's movement Maria stopped and turned, a half smile to her mother and a look of puzzlement that there was another person here as well. Then a burst of radiance as recognition hit her face, frozen by a flash of uncertainty, self-conscious in the moment.

He could not help it, Jimmy just grinned at her with a forlorn puppy grin, completely lost in the moment. Suddenly they were all laughing to hide their mixed joy and embarrassment.

Alison stepped forward to break the moment. "I think you have met before, but this is Jimmy. He has come to see you, to thank you for helping him the other day."

Another flash of embarrassment by both of them, but Alison continued on. "He brought me a lovely strawberry-cream cake, so I invited him to join us for afternoon tea". Then, addressing Maria, Alison said, "Perhaps, dear, you would help me set up the tea things."

Charles stepped forward to shake Jimmy's hand, a man of power appraising his daughter's visitor with a searching look. Charles had felt the electricity pass between Maria and this man. Focusing on the scars and half healed cuts on Jimmy's face, he said "Hah, a man with a penchant for trouble, by the look of that face. Better that than some namby pamby who runs away. Come with me son, I want to show you something while the ladies organise the tea things."

Jimmy followed him across the house. They stepped out of open double doors onto a sandstone paved terrace that looked down a steep hill to a little cove of water, indented slightly into the steep rocky hillside. Near the shore a small boat was anchored, blue hull, white masts and white furled sails. Painted on the stern in bright red letters was "Alison-Heather-Maria".

"Named after the three women I love the best" the man said. "I had it built soon after Maria was born. I have taught them all to sail in her. Perhaps one day you will come for a sail in her too."

Tea was served, all sitting around a table on the sandstone terrace. Suddenly, both shy and not sure where to begin, Jimmy and Maria half looked at each other from the corners of their eyes, but avoided direct eye contact. Alison and Charles carried the conversation and entertained with light banter from town. The cake was declared a great success. Maria described her purchases for the shop, hesitant and self-conscious.

Then Alison came in, "Do you know who Jimmy is? His grandmother was my dear friend, Sophia, who lived in that lovely little cottage in Smith St. You know, whose husband died in the wreck of the Adelie in that awful storm far out in the Southern Ocean in 71.

She died in January this year. She is buried next to Tom and Mary, where she too can look out to the sea."

Jimmy felt his eyes move to the far horizon as a wistful look came over his face. It was as if this broke the spell. Maria looked at him with sudden softness, the embarrassment gone. "You must still be sad, I can feel that you miss her, even now," she said.

Then, with a flash of brightness returning to her face, "Would you show me her house? It must not be too far from the Exchange Hotel where I work."

It was time for Alison and Charles to leave them to sit alone. They both excused themselves and went off.

Suddenly Jimmy remembered. He still had not given Maria the brooch. He said. "I bought something for you to say 'Thank You' for the other day." He stood up to pull the little package out of his pocket and walked over, next to her, to hand it to her.

She stood up to face him, holding out her hand to take it, all the while looking at him with those steady serious eyes. Then, with great delicacy, she carefully peeled back the paper and opened the small cloth bag.

When she looked up there a great fondness in her manner, "Thank you, oh thank you. This is the most beautiful present I have ever been given." She reached up, on tiptoes, and kissed him gently on the cheek.

For a second they stood facing each other. Then she took his hand and led him down the path to the cove. When they reached the beach she turned to face him again, a luminous light in her eyes.

This time she came right up next to him, her body touching his and reached up for his face, then pulled herself up and kissed him, ever so slowly and gently, on the mouth. "I so wanted to do that when I saw your poor hurt face the other day but I made myself stop. Today I just had to do it."

He put his arms around her and held her too him. She felt so small and soft and vulnerable against him, as her body melted in to him and she clung to him and pressed herself against him. He wanted to kiss her back, and lifted her face again towards his.

But her eyes were brimming with tears and she stifled a sob. "Oh Jimmy, there is something I have to tell you. I am so scared you won't like me after it. I can't help myself from loving you and I want you to love me too. But I can't pretend everything is alright and tell lies with you."

Jimmy looked at her with puzzlement and went as if to brush it aside.

"No I mean it, just listen," she said.

She took a deep breath and sat down on a rock. She made him sit next to her, not touching, just far enough away so she saw all of him clearly. Looking intently into his eyes, she began.

"I was born a long time after my brother and sister and they seemed grown up from when I remember. They were so clever and good at things. Heather was tall and really beautiful, with long dark hair. She was very clever at school, and she was so good at making things. She could make beautiful clothes and she could draw. By the time I was at school she was already selling her clothes for money. Everyone would compare her to Grandma Hannah, who was a famous dressmaker, and say she was just as good. People were forever saying how wonderful she was. Before long she had opened a big millinery shop in the town. She was so beautiful, she always dressed in beautiful clothes and she had lots of money for jewellery, buying things and going out.

"My brother John was just the same, good at everything; school, sailing, making things. He often helped Dad with his new electric machines, and he mixed with lots of other clever, handsome boys. These boys swooned over Heather, always wanting to ask her out or seek her advice. She was always nice to me her small kid sister, and John was just the same.

"But, after a while, I started to feel angry. Why they should get so much attention and so many good things. I felt I was just a plain little mouse; not very clever in lessons, not beautiful or successful. I did not want to be called 'Nice, Good Maria', while they laughed at my silliness and dullness.

"It was not that Mum and Dad favoured them, or did not give me things or love me. But I felt the ugly duckling alongside two beautiful swans. I began to behave badly, to get in trouble at school, be rude to teachers, argue with Mum, tell her she was stupid and what would she know.

"One day, when I was fifteen, I went to a party in Sydney with my family, at the Governor's house. There was a man about ten years older than me. He had been a soldier and sailed on ships. His father was some Lord in England. He was nice to me and danced with me for half the night. He made me feel so special. Mum and Dad were happy to see me having a good time and did not pay too much attention.

"At the end of the night he made me secretly promise to meet him after school the next day, and then the day after. He was witty and charming and would take me to quiet places where we could sit and talk, just the two of us. He would bring me little gifts and hold my hand. And then he would start to kiss me. Before long he was doing things to me, when we met, that Mum and Dad would have got angry about, touching me, stroking me in private places, 'helping me enjoy my beautiful womanly gifts', he said.

"One day he arranged for me to come to his rooms in town. There he undressed me and made love to me on his bed. I knew it was wrong but he was so charming and I thought I loved him and he loved me. Next week he was sailing away to Malaya, so he made me promise to come with him.

"On the night, just before the ship sailed and the other sailors came on board, he sneaked me into his cabin. So I sailed away with him. I left a short note for my parents, just to tell them I had gone away, nothing more, that was all. Before they discovered it I was gone.

"I stayed in his cabin and, for a few days, no one knew I was there, but then I got found out. The captain was angry but it was too late to put me ashore and anyway, the Lord, his father, owned the ship. So there really wasn't anything the captain could do.

"We called at Malaya for a few days and then sailed on to Hong Kong. By then my man had become bored with me. He even offered to let the other men try me out, 'sample my wares', he said.

"I locked myself in the cabin and would not let anyone in. When I finally came out I brought a knife and, when one man tried to grab me, I cut him. After that they left me alone, but when we came to Hong Kong two sailors crept up on me, grabbed me and tied my hands. I heard them say that 'his Lordship', that's what they called him, 'had paid them money to get rid of me, because I was an ungrateful hellcat.'

"So they took me into the town and left me with a madam, Mrs Chan, saying I was a wild one and, if she could tame me, she could have me for nothing. By now it was two months after we had left Sydney and I knew I was going to have a baby, but no one else could tell.

"First Mrs Chan was kind to me and tried to get me to go with men as a favour to her. But I would not. Then she got angry and they fed me drugs so I was half asleep and could not stop it when the men did it. After a while I did not care anymore. So I would just lie there and pretend it was not real while they did their things with me. But I hated it.

"After a couple months Mrs Chan saw that a baby was coming and she did not want to lose me. So, one night, she made me take some medicine, it tasted awful, opium I think. Then three big ladies came into my room and undressed me and held my legs apart. One stuck a long needle thing up inside me, which hurt so much. She poked it around until blood came out, then they left me. A little later I had violent cramps and there, between my legs, was a tiny baby, the size of my finger. I was so sad, so angry and so ashamed, all together.

"They thought I was asleep with the medicine and had not locked the door. So I put on my clothes and ran out in to the street. A kind old man brought me to an English gentleman's house. His wife came to the door and knew, almost at once, what had happened."

Maria had barely drawn a breath as she said all this and her eyes had never left his, and his eyes never left hers. But he felt as though he had been hit by a steam hammer. For a second he broke her stare, he had to think.

She let out a muffled sob. As he looked back at her, her shoulders were shaking. Soon she was sobbing and sobbing.

Jimmy felt too as if his heart would break, but it was not anger at her, just a sharing of such a profound grief. He could feel the broken place that ran through her, much bigger but like the hurt inside him.

He moved right next to her and put his arm around her and held her close, gently stroking her hair, feeling her body convulse against him. "Dear Maria, dear Maria, it's alright, how could I like you less for this."

She looked at him with a look that spoke of a mixture of fear and joyous amazement, as if she was scared that he could still like her but so, so wanted it to be true.

Then she took another deep breath. "I must finish, I will never be able to say it again. Even Mum and Dad don't know the half of it."

She continued. "I got very sick for a few weeks, they said it was blood poisoning from the dirty needle, but eventually I got better, and the family who cared for me were very kind. They wanted me to stay on with them and write to let my parents know I was safe and then send me back to them. But I was so ashamed.

"Finally I agreed to write a short note to tell my parents I was alright, if they would book me a passage to Melbourne. I so, so wanted to go back to Australia, but I could not bear to face my parents or for them to really know what had happened.

"So I came to Melbourne. I found a job in a dress shop, sewing hems and lace, something that Heather had taught me. I stayed there for a year. Once I tried to write my Mum a letter, as I so wanted to see her and come home. But I could not find courage to post it. So I threw it in the river.

"One day I was doing an errand, delivering a dress. The boy, whose sister it was for, answered the door. He was someone from my school before and recognised me. He asked me how I came to be in Melbourne and I mumbled some silly reason, but I don't think he believed me. It turned out he told his mother. She sent a letter to my own mother saying she had seen me in Melbourne, working at a dress shop, asking if everything was alright?

"A month later, just as I was finishing work, there were Mum and Dad waiting for me, standing outside the shop. I cried and cried and they held me tight and finally I could tell them some of what happened, about the man and going to Hong Kong, but not about Mrs Chan and the baby and the needle. They brought me home and showed me they loved me more than ever, and now, after another year, I start to feel better, and be able to help my Mum in the shop and even serve in a parlour.

"But, when the men look at me in that funny way, I know what they want to do to me and I get all scared inside and want to run away. So I act angry with them just to show I am not scared.

"Then you come and look at me with those big sad eyes, and that puppy dog face. I see that you are scarred and broken a bit too, and I can't help but love you a little and want to hold you and make you better.

"Then I see you lying in the corner and your face is a mess, and the men tell me they caught you cheating and what you got serves you right. I have to help you and as I help you I just want to kiss and love you."

Finally she stopped talking, all her words were said, and she felt like a broken kernel with just a tiny seed of hope. Even if he did not really love her she had told the worst and told it all. In the telling a bad part of it was gone.

But he did not leave her, he just sat there looking at her and smiling his sad happy smile. "If I wanted I could not stop loving you, even if it cut my heart out."

She moved in again, close to him and he held her and he held her, and still he held her, as the light slowly faded out to the west. In the dusk they walked up to the house, knowing that their souls were joined and their new life together begun.

Alison knew in a glance that all was well and rushed over and hugged them both tightly. "Welcome to our family Jimmy," was all she said.

To Charles she said, "I want to sit and talk with Maria a small while. Can you bring Jimmy up to the town in the carriage?"

For most of the way Charles and Jimmy rode together in silence. Then finally, as they came close to the town lights, Charles said. "Seeing how you look at Maria brings to mind how I first looked at Alison all those many years ago."

Then, a minute later, he said. "Where is it to, lad?"

Jimmy started from his reverie. First he thought to direct him to the boarding house in the docks. Then he said. "My Mum and Dad live in that big house on Montague, near the corner with Darling. I have much news for them. Could you drop me there, please?"

Back at the house Alison sat with her arm around Maria. First they sat in silence. Then Maria turned to her with shining eyes and said. "Oh Mum, I told him all and at first I thought my heart would break. But he just sat there and listened and looked at me with those big sad eyes, and then he put his arms around me and held me tight and I knew it would be alright.

"O Mum, I just want to burst with happiness that he doesn't hate me. I want to make him so happy too. I have been so scared since you invited him to visit at the shop, but it is better now."

Next day Maria worked with Alison at the shop. In the mid-afternoon, getting near to closing time, the door opened. There was Jimmy, flushed with exertion and holding a flower for them both. He looked at Maria and said. "You said you wanted to see the house. I was hoping when you finish for the day that you would come with me and I could show you."

Maria wanted to stay and help her mother lock up but Alison shooed them. So they walked along, Maria lightly holding his arm.

Jimmy had spent all day fixing, cleaning, tidying and sweeping. He had enlisted his mother and father to help as well. His Dad had called on Jim Roberts from down the road and, before the sun was well up, they were at it. His Dad set too, with hammer and nails inside, fixing loose boards and patching holes, while Jim and Jimmy worked at the outside, cleaning and straightening gutters, re nailing shingles, trimming branches and removing the rubbish. Rosie cleaned the floors and polished the windows. By lunch their work was done and they left Jimmy to do the finishing touches. He decided to start all over and re-clean everything, just to be double sure. By three o'clock the house shone like a new pin. All it needed was a new coat of paint and some fresh flowers to grow in the front garden.

With aching muscles and raw hands, he headed up the hill to the shop. Passing Mrs Jones' house he saw she had several red roses in full bloom in the front yard. A quick jump over the fence and he picked the two best.

As he was leaving he looked over his shoulder. She was looking at him and wagging her finger. "Ah, Jimmy Williams, tis for ye new sweetheart, tis it? Tis talk of the town. Mind you tell her they are my very best."

Coming back along the street all the neighbours were out to see. "Good day, Jimmy," "How ye doing Mr Jimmy," "Coming back to the old house, so I see." Jimmy doffed his hat and Maria smiled and nodded politely. Jimmy opened the door with a flourish and they stepped inside.

Coming into the passage, Jimmy steered her to the front room with the fireplace. "My grandmother, Sophia's, favourite room", he said. "She would hold court here and all the neighbourhood gentlemen and ladies would call to visit. Often I would sit with her for hours, just quietly telling stories and reminisces, while we watched the life pass in the street."

Maria came up to him and lay her head on his chest. This will be our new Sophie's room. When you make a girl baby inside me I will call her Sophie and this will be her room.

She walked over to the window and pulled closed the curtains. In the half-light she unbuttoned her dress and pulled him against her breast, then placed her hands under his shirt and stroked his back and belly. "Will you love me now, and fill me with you."

On a rug, on the timber floor, they joined their bodies just as they had joined their souls in that last evening. Two months later he placed a gold ring on her finger in the Catholic Church at the top of the hill. While he cared little for any church he knew that this was what his grandmother, Sophia, would have wanted.

As they lay together, in their Balmain house on their wedding night, two months later, Maria placed his hand on the soft skin of her belly. "Already I know that a new life has begun in there," she said.

Chapter 15 - 1900-1901 - Plague and Celebrations

As Maria and Jimmy settled into their married life in Smith St there was much ado in Sydney. It was like two cities, those who lived in the big houses and those who lived in squats, often ten to a little house, and then some, like themselves, in the middle. Down around the White Bay docks, where the poor people lived, the stench was awful. Often these streets were soiled with excrement. Sometimes beggars from there would walk along their street, seeking little things, though mostly the police kept them to their part.

But all mixed at the football games at Birchgrove Oval, where all shouted together for the team with the orange and black stripes. Maria and Jimmy would go to all the games. Sometimes they would go and stand with the nobs, where Mike and Rosie stood and, at times, Charles and Alison came there too. But best Jimmy liked to go with his friends from the docks. Maria loved the wild rough way they all cheered and heckled

"Doon you know how to catch the ball you yoosless Mick. Give it to that Kiwi winger there, at least he runs straight, Hit him hard man, knock him flat, clobber him, doon let that Pom run over you."

Many had met Maria while working at the Exchange. They knew better than to cross her and also knew that she did not give a toss about all their cussing and swearing.

The plague was sweeping the city but yet to be seen in Balmain. They said rats spread it. These were plentiful at the bottom of the hill where most workers lived. Balmain lived in fear that it would come soon. Jimmy was scrupulous keeping rats away from the house. He set traps, he had a big tabby cat he fed out the back and he always made sure there were no scraps lying around. But they knew it could come anytime and before long there was a case and then there was another, and soon new rows of graves stood in Leichardt cemetery.

For Jimmy and Maria neither this, nor the hard life of their friends, nor anything else, could spoil their happiness. Each Sunday they went to church and gave their alms. Whenever they saw poor people in the street they tried to help them, even if their stink was terrible. They knew that they both could have been there too. They listened, with gratitude filling their hearts, as the priest exhorted that charity begins at home.

Maria's belly, which at first had hardly shown, was now there for all to see. The bigger it grew the prouder Jimmy was. She could have sworn he most liked her to wear dresses which showed it when they went out walking.

Sophie came early, just 6 months after they were married. She was small, but perfectly formed; dark hair like her grandmother, Rosie, but her eyes came from Maria. Even though not big she was full of fight and sucked her mother's breast strongly. Maria marvelled at how perfect she was and the wonder of her birth after what had been done to her insides. But since she met Jimmy she had never doubted it would be thus, that each could repair the other's broken body and make it whole again.

Sometimes she wondered at her lust for him. After all those brutal men she never thought she would find such pleasure in a man again. But he had only to look at her, like he did on that first afternoon in the house, and she was overwhelmed by her desire for him. Even after he lay back, spent, she wanted him to do it all again, to again feel his body move in her and quench her need. And he was just the same. Whenever he looked at her and she looked back at him it was like a fire was lit in his body, so powerful was his desire for her, in the boat, on the beach, walking in the forest. They laughed together at how quickly the passion could come on and at all the places and times in which it was enjoyed. Even big with Sophie it was the same, an ache, desire, then fire, ecstasy and the release.

Now there was much work to be done. They repainted the house in the lemon yellow of the frangipani centres, they replanted the garden, they built a cot for Sophie. Alison's business was booming with work for both of them. Jimmy spent many hours there; serving customers, collecting orders. Now and then came special days when they went off to Sydney town together, to search the boats, stalls and shops for new special gift items.

As 1900 drew to a close they celebrated their second Christmas together, their first with baby Sophie. After church at St Augustine's they walked to East Balmain where they ate a roast turkey dinner with Alison and Charles and all their other children and grandchildren.

With their baby being the newest and smallest they were treated as most important guests, with special gifts for Sophie; a music box from her grandmother to soothe her to sleep, a boat on a string to hang over her cot from her grandfather, a set of beautiful hand sewn clothes from her aunt, a cup and plate engraved with her name from her uncle, and little toys from all her cousins. Maria saw, with startling clarity, that this was what was best in life, this simple pleasure of being part of a family growing and sharing life and love together.

Now that her hurt was past she felt as if everything was a special gift from God and wondered with amazement at how she had reached this place. She knew that without the pain she would never have met Jimmy and that he and her had something even better together than her sister and brother did, although they seemed happy too. The closest to match it was her Mum and Dad but, by coming past the pain and mending each other, it made it even better for her and Jimmy.

That night they walked back to the big house in Montague Street, to be with Rosie and Michael. It was again a special family occasion. But here, as well as family, there were many other guests. All were agog with the news of the Federation, the start of Australia, soon to become its own country, not just a group of colonies.

There was only a week left until the big parade where it became official in Hyde Park. Up to now this had largely passed Maria and Jimmy by. Now they felt this excitement catch them too. After they came home together, late into the night, and tucked little Sophie into her cot, they sat on the front verandah, in the night stillness, inhaling fragrance of the frangipani.

Jimmy turned to Maria and said, "You know I used to think Federation stuff was all a load or rubbish and had naught to do with me. I reckoned the way my Mum and Dad banging on about it, it was all was just cobblers.

"But that was before I grew up and took on responsibility. Now I feel I understand why our country needs to grow up too and leave old mother England behind. It's just the same as how we can't live with your Mum and Dad, even though they have plenty of room and would love to invite us, and I think they are the best people in the world. But this is our life and we have to live it for ourselves."

For Maria these words made so much sense, it was almost exactly the same ideas she had, first starting with the lunch and then becoming clear in her mind with the dinner. This was their time now and their country's too.

Jimmy went on, almost as if apologetic for saying so much. "I've been thinking. You know how I mostly hate marches and such. But I really think we should go anyway, it like us and the country saying the same thing together."

So they went, holding up Sophie to let her see as they stood along Park Street, watching as the grand parade passed them by. They felt so proud seeing their country grown up alongside them. When the parade was over they gave Sophie to Maria's parents, who had stood alongside them.

Then, holding hands and laughing with the fun of it all, they walked around the city, part of a vast throng of happy people, differences forgotten and joined for one special day. As the night came they found themselves swept along with the crowd, moving down George St to Circular Quay where the whole town was a party. So they joined the others; cheering and dancing, till the night was past and the new day had come.

As the weeks passed it seemed that something was changed forever for both them and their new country. They really were Mr and Mrs Williams, the family, and their country had its own new name that everyone was using, more and more, Australia, and they who belonged to it, Australians.

1901 rolled along, and now they were busy again with their lives. Jimmy seemed to have a flair to match her Mum at spotting beautiful things, and Maria realised she had this talent from her Mum as well, that instinctive knowledge of beauty and that ability to see it, as through other eyes. She could look at a person and know, almost before asking, what they needed, what would suit them and what they most desired. She had often thought her Mum a bit fey, a mind reader or mystic. Now she could feel these same skills growing in herself; a thread running between her and her mother.

Still Jimmy felt he needed to do more; it was as if she had unlocked all his restless energy and given it focus. When he could find time he worked with his father and Jim in the building firm, which again prospered. He took great delight at the texture and form of things his hands made. One day he showed her a ceiling he had made, fashioned from a mould in the workshop, now suspended in a grand house. It was made of pressed metal, worked into exquisite shapes, flowers, leaves and little wave like patterns flowing across the plaster.

"Did you fashion all that yourself," she said. "It's a work of art in plaster."

He nodded shyly.

"Could you make us a ceiling like that, to go into our sitting room. When I look at what is there now, after seeing this, it seems rather plain." Two weeks later it was in place. Now, on hot afternoons, as Maria felt drowsy and her belly swelled again with a second child, she lay back and stared in delight at his truly wonderful workmanship, her mind transported into the picture he had made especially for her.

Chapter 16 - 1905-1907 – Balmain's Children

Sophie raced down the street like a wild urchin, dark hair streaming behind. Chasing her was Matty McNeil, her best friend, almost two years older, their birthdays only a month apart. Today was a special day. It was her birthday. Her Mum had read her a story about someone who was five and how grown up they were, and now she was five too. For a present today her Dad gave her a three wheeler trike; he had made it himself. It had pedals and round wooden wheels and a basket on the back to carry her work things. He had painted it bright red, her favourite colour.

Tonight there would be a party, and her Grandma Alison and Grandpa Charles would be there. Grandma Rosie and Grandpa Mick would have come too, but they were away on a trip, gone to somewhere with a long name that she couldn't quite remember it. They would be back soon and perhaps they would bring her some presents too.

She loved her Grandma Rosie too but Gran Alison was best. She could tell when she looked into your eyes what you were really thinking. And at times, when Mummy and Gran Alison and her all looked at each other together, they all knew what each was thinking. It sounded a bit complicated (now that was a big word for a little girl – or so her Daddy often said), but sometimes it was easier to understand things like that than explain them. With the three of them it was like you could pass your thoughts across to each other and they could see them too.

The only other person she could do that with, just a tiny little bit, was Matty, but he was too nice and sometimes she did not want him to see what she was thinking, most especially if she was trying to trick him or be mean. Plus, she wanted to marry him when she grew up. She certainly did not want him to know that, or perhaps he would forget to ask her, ever so politely.

Matty headed home, time for him to do his chores and get dressed before he came back to her party. Inside, her Mummy was bathing baby Rachel and Alexander was playing with Daddy, sort of helping him hang decorations for the party. Alexander was almost four. Even though he was almost as tall as her she could run much faster. There was a beetle named Alexander too but didn't think it could run very fast either. And she had a favourite Great Uncle, Alexander, Gran Alison's brother. He had half black and half grey hair which stuck out from his head and he did the funniest things and made lots of jokes. When he came to visit he would teach her tricks and make her laugh. He had promised that when she turned six her would bring her to the zoo to see the lions and elephants – thinking about that she could barely wait for her next birthday, a whole year away. But for now today's party was the most exciting thing ever.

She heard her father call her name to come for the bath. She did not want to come inside, but then inside meant getting ready for the party, so that might make it happen sooner. There was a big cast iron bath in the wash room and her Dad had filled it up, almost to her knees, with warm water. Alexander was already in it playing with the soap and a duck. She was too grown up now to play with the duck and she really thought she was too big to share a bath with Alexander, but perhaps that could begin tomorrow, after she had finished turning five. So they both washed and played.

In five minutes their Dad came in with two towels. He told them to stand up, grabbed each under the arms and whisked them out. Before they knew it they were wrapped in towels and going to their bedrooms. It was cold, but it was winter, and so her Dad had the fire lit in her room. On her bed was her favourite pink dress, the one with ruffles and long sleeves which her Aunty Heather had given her, and with it was a pink ribbon for her hair.

She was half way through brushing out her wet hair when there was a knock on the front door. She peeked through and saw it was Granny Al. Sophie flung herself into her arms. Daddy and Mummy were there too and everyone was welcomed into the sitting room, where another fire was going. Except for her own room, with the pink fireplace and cosy chair next to the bed, it was her most favourite room.

At times, when she was tired, she would lie with her head on her Daddy's lap and gaze up at the beautiful ceiling he had made. It was like living inside a picture, she could see herself running through all the flowers and leaves and waves he had placed there. He told her he had done it specially to make her Mummy happy. She did not know who she loved the best in the whole world, her Daddy or her Mummy or her Gran Alison. Perhaps it did not matter and she could love them all the same.

She climbed on her Gran's lap in front of the fire, handing her the brush and ribbons. "Please, will you brush and do my hair and make me look pretty. I like it the way you do it the best."

Alison looked at her small grand-daughter, like a little changeling, with dark hair, but with those eyes of her Maria, like her own eyes, which her Da had said were the same as those of her Mum, Hannah. She had an instant powerful sense of life's continuity. She saw clearly that this small girl would hold a special place in it; she too was one who shared the deep wisdom of a memory keeper. She gave Sophie her own special secret smile and brushed away at her hair with love embedded in every stroke.

A year passed; it was time for another birthday party. This time it was at Grandma Alison and Grandpa Charles place. All her cousins were there and some other friends too, of course including Matty. But she was a bit mad at him today. Her older cousin Elizabeth was there and Matty was talking to her more than anyone else.

Well, she would show him. She went and knocked on Grandma's Al's bedroom door. Gran opened it, dressed in a wrap. "Oh Sophie, my pet, do you want to come in. I was just fixing my make-up and hair, perhaps you could help." She handed her a silver necklace, saying, "Could you do up the clasp at the back. It is getting hard for my clumsy fingers."

Sophie saw her take out a small pale blue-green perfume bottle, covered in beautiful silver patterns, just like the waves on the sea. Gran touched her finger to the top and touched a dab behind each ear.

Sophie's watched her grandmother turn it in her hand. A sparkling blue eye set into the silver came into view. Her eyes grew wide as she looked at it. "Gran, that is so lovely. Please tell me where it came from?"

Gran looked at her with watchful eyes. "First I will put a dab behind your ears. I used to do this to your Mum too when she was a little girl."

As Gran touched her skin with the tip of her finger, Sophie felt a smell flow over her. It was like a mixture of apple blossoms and summer sun, with a hint of the smell of ocean breeze and a shady forest. It made her feel happy all the way through. It was her mother's smell and Gran's smell, but so much more as well.

"This is the place where I keep all my happy memories," said her Gran.

Sophie knew it was no ordinary bottle but something really special.

Gran said, "I was thinking that one day soon it should be yours. First I must tell you its story, like I told your mother a long time ago. After I told your Mum I still needed it for myself to put more happy memories in. Now it is full, almost to overflowing. But there is no time today. So it will be my gift to you when you turn seven. Then I will tell you its story.

The year flew by. It was mostly happy but sometimes sad for Sophie. Her Daddy and Mummy loved her, just as ever and were talking about having another baby once they built a room on the back of the house. But they were busy a lot. So it seemed the room and baby would have to wait.

Rachel was now two. She had moved into Sophie's room a little while ago, too big now for the cot in her Mummy's room. At first Sophie was cross, because it meant there was no longer any room for her favourite cosy chair, they called it Sophia's chair. But then she was happy again, she could tell her sister some girly things she could not say to Matty or Alexander, and she loved to sit on her bed with Rachel and read her stories from the books she brought home from school. Sometimes Rachel would fall asleep. At first this made Sophie mad, because no one would fall asleep when they were really interested, but then she remembered that Rachel was just a little girl and little girls needed more sleep. So now, when it happened, she would carry Rachel over to her own bed, tuck her in and give her a kiss, just like her Mummy, or sometimes her Daddy, did.

But Matty made her sad, he was eight and seemed to have decided Sophie, still six, was not grown up enough. He often ignored her and went and played with older boys who lived in the next street. Even when he talked to her he mostly seemed cross. He said that his Mummy and Daddy shouted at each other a lot and sometimes his Dad would go off to the pub and come home so drunk he could hardly walk. The next day his Mummy would shout at him even more.

Still, now that Alexander was more grown up, she could mostly play with him and they could have great games of hide and seek in the garden. Also, now she and Alexander were both going to school, they could walk there together. Often Alexander would carry her bag as well as his own, just like Daddy did with Mummy.

Before she knew it Sophie was turning seven, and it was coming up to her birthday party again. This time it was held at Granny Rosie's place. All her friends from school came and they played lots of games.

Granny Alison was there too, but because Sophie was so busy with her friends she did not have much time to talk to her. Mostly Gran just sat with Grandpa Charles, holding his hand and talking quietly to him. At times she smiled at Sophie and, a few times, she got up and talked to others.

Sophie hoped that, when she was grown up and married to Matty, that he would sit and talk to her like that and look at her in the same way Grandpa Charles looked at Gran Alison. It was like to him her Gran was just as young and pretty as the day Grandpa first met her, even though they were both starting to look quite old and their hair was going grey.

At the end of the night her Gran came up to her, before she left, and gave her a special hug and kiss. Then she held her face in both her hands. "Sophie, I have not forgotten my promise to you to give you my perfume bottle for a special present. Perhaps, on Saturday, you can come and visit me and we will have a picnic together. Then I will tell you its story."

When Saturday morning came Sophie said to her Mum. "I have to visit Gran today, she wants to give me a special present, I think it is her perfume bottle; you know the one she puts all her happy memories into."

Maria picked her up and hugged her. "Oh, Darling of course you must go. I remember when I was little she used to put perfume from it on me and it would make me feel warm and happy all over. After I had been away and came back all sad, one day she sat with me while I cried. When I finished, she took out that bottle and touched my tears and put a tiny drop inside. She said that even though it was a sad memory, one day, while it was still inside the bottle, it would turn into a happy memory. That's what happened when you came along. I am so glad she wants you to have it."

So Sophie skipped down the road and before long she was at her Gran's house. It was just her and her Gran there today, all by themselves.

Gran brought her out to a small table on the edge of the terrace. There were two chairs and a little cake with strawberries, just big enough for two, and two glasses of lemonade. Sitting in the middle of the table was a little present wrapped in gold and silver paper with a blue bow.

Alison, her finger touching the wrapping, said, "This present is for you, my dear Sophie. Before you open it I must first tell you its story."

She told Sophie the story that had come to her from long ago, of how the bottle was passed, over hundreds of years, from mother to daughter and granddaughter until, after all those years, it was filled with good memories.

She went on, "When I was a little girl, about as big as you are now, my Mummy died, and I was so sad. Soon after, my brother died too. I was even sadder and my Daddy was very sad too. He had to go away on a long trip. Before he went he gave me this bottle as a special present from my Mummy, Hannah, even though she was not there anymore. He said it was given to my Mummy as a special present from Gran Mary. Gran Mary loved my Mummy and me just the same as your Mummy loves you.

"Next day, after my Daddy was gone, I showed the bottle to Gran Mary. She told me how, for all the years she had it, she had put her own happy memories inside it. Then, when she gave it to my Mummy, Hannah, she also put her own special memories in there; things like when I made her laugh, or when Daddy made her cross and then hugged her and it made it better.

"So, each night while my Daddy was away, I would take it out and smell it, and sometimes I would put a tiny drop on my cheek, and sometimes, when I cried, I would put a tear inside. Each time I held it, it was like Mummy was sitting next to me and, when I smelled it, it was like a warm summer breeze making me happy.

"Then, when I was grown up, and Charles and my babies came, I put those happy memories in it too. Now it is full of all my memories and it is time for you to start putting your happy memories in there too. Some will be about your friends, some about your Mummy and Daddy and your brother and sister, some will even be sad things. But, after they have stayed in there for a long time, most of them will turn happy too.

"Now I am old and one day I will be gone. But you will have this bottle to help remember. So, my dear Sophie, now it belongs to you and it is full of my love for you," she said, passing her the bottle.

They ate their strawberry cake and drank their lemonade. When it was finished her Gran said, "I want to show you something, a place I have not been to for a long, long time. Perhaps I will not be able to find it, because I was only about as big as you last time I went there. I want you to come with me and we will try to find it. First you have to put on some old clothes and walking shoes, I am sure we will have a pair in the cupboard to fit."

So off they went with her Gran leading the way and carrying a little bag on her shoulder. It felt like they walked a long way, at first along streets and then through bush, climbing up and down over rocks. Sophie was amazed; even though her Gran looked old she could climb almost as good as she and Matty could. Even when they had walked a long way, her Gran's legs did not seem to get tired the way her own legs did.

At last the came to a rocky headland poking into the sea. Her Gran led her along a rough path, like a wallaby path, around the side of the hill. They climbed up over a couple of big rocks. Behind the rocks and a bush, where no one who did not know could see it, Gran showed her a small opening into the hill, just big enough for her and Gran to squeeze through.

Inside was a little cave, barely big enough to stand up in or lie down. It had sand on the floor, and light came in through a gap in some rocks, up high. In one corner was a small wooden chest, a couple bottles and some other things.

A smile lit up her Gran's face. "Imagine, it's still all here. It has been so long, but I did not want to come here again without another little girl to share it with, and to see it like I used to see it.

"Perhaps I could have brought your Mum or Heather but there never seemed to be time, or maybe the moment just was not right."

They sat on the floor and unpacked the bag. While they ate cakes and oranges Alison told Sophie the story of her little aboriginal friend, Ruthie, all those many years ago.

She told she first met Ruthie soon after her mother. Hannah, had died and how Ruthie's father and mother had died at the same time with the flu that came in on the boat, so the only family Ruthie had left was her aunt, two cousins and her grandfather Jimmy. Their friendship was made strong because of this shared pain Alison told of how she visited Ruthie's family, feasted on kangaroo, and met Ruthie's grandfather. Then she told of how she and Ruthie used to go exploring, collect treasures and bring them to the cave, then imagine adventures with them, going to faraway places and doing amazing things, then how this friendship ended when her family left Balmain, how her Dad made her come and live in Newcastle, and ho w she really missed Ruthie but never saw her again. She had tried to find out what happened to her when she came back for holidays with Tom and Mary, but no one knew where she was gone. Once she had walked to the place where Ruthie had lived, but no one lived there anymore. Only a couple broken house walls with the roof fallen in and a few empty bottles remained.

So at last she was back in the cave where she last saw Ruthie. She said she was happy to share this place with Sophie, even though there was a tear in her eye, which trickled down her cheek.

Sophie took out her perfume bottle. With great seriousness she touched it to Gran's cheek, where the tear was, put it in the bottle and she replaced the lid.

Suddenly they were both laughing, and her Gran said, "That's just what Ruthie and I would do, we would sit here and tell stories and then suddenly we would start laughing. Then, later at night, I would put that laughter into the perfume bottle to keep our happiness safe."

Sophie thought of one more thing she wanted to ask her Gran. "Gran, at times when you look at me and I look at you and we both look at Mum, it is like we are all sharing our thoughts together and we can see what each is feeling. I like it when that happens, because we can share happy thoughts together. So why did you give this bottle to me and not to Mummy?"

Her Gran looked at her intently, "Your Mummy looks much the same on the outside as me, and on the outside you look different to me. But on the inside it is you who is most like me and your Mummy is more different.

"We can all share our thoughts, but for your Mummy it is different. There is a place inside her, like a broken place, where pain lives. The happy memories in the bottle cannot take that pain away, like it can with you and me. When I first saw your Daddy, he was standing at the grave of your great grandmother, Sophia. I could feel in him the same sad and broken place as is in my Maria. Together they heal each other and make each other whole. Even when they fight, which I know they do sometimes, together they are stronger that all my other children. Maria and Jimmy tell me this each time I see them look at one another. So together they do not need the perfume bottle, apart it cannot really help them.

"For you and me it is easier, for them it is harder. But you can help find and fix that sad place which your mother has, through sharing nice thoughts with her. That is why I have given you the bottle, so that when I am gone you can still help me make her happy, wherever I am and wherever you are."

At last all the talking was done so they packed to leave. As they reached the entrance her Grandma stopped and put her hand to her head.

"I almost forgot."

She went over to the small wooden chest and opened it. From inside she pulled out a wooden bowl and passed it to Sophie. It was a little wider than Sophie's hand with her fingers open and half a long again. On the outside were patterns, some painted in ochre and some cut into the wood. One looked like a picture of an echidna.

Alison said, "Isn't it funny how one forgets, like I almost did now. This belonged to Ruthie and she left it here. It was the only thing she had that her father had made. That echidna pattern is her father's totem which he carved into the wood with a burning stick. I thought that she'd come and get it after I went away and take it back. But it is still her so it must be she never did.

"I somehow feel it needs to go back to its rightful owner, I don't know if we can ever find Ruthie after all those years but perhaps we can find some other person from her family to give it to, perhaps one of the aboriginal people who live around here will know something about what happened to the people from the camp that used to be at the end of Blackwattle Bay.

What do you think, Sophie? Perhaps if we all ask around someone will know. I'll tell you what, I will put a sign in my shop, you ask in your school class, and I can ask Charles and Maria and Jimmy to ask around too. If we all try there is still a chance we can find someone who remembers and can say what happened way back then and tell us where they went.

Sophie nodded and passed the bowl back to Alison. As it left her hand she felt this small bowl tugging at her. Her mind sensed another small girl, who was part echidna, saying, "Leave me here. This is where I want to stay. All those who made me have gone. Now I belong here. It is a good place for me to stay, my underground burrow which keeps me safe and warm.

Sophie could feel her Gran share her mind picture, the way they shared other thoughts. So they put the bowl back in the box and closed the lid, knowing it was not for them to take it away.

As they came outside Gran carefully looked around, as if to make sure no one could see them before they came out into view.

As they walked back along the path she said to Sophie, "I want this to be our secret, just for you and me. When we were little Ruthie and I made a promise that we would not tell anyone else. I have told you now but that is alright. I know now Ruthie understands, since she just spoke to you. If you want you can come again and bring one special friend, but apart from that it should stay secret, sometimes secrets are best."

Sophie nodded her head.

When they got back to her Gran's house and changed their clothes, her Gran said, "I will bring you up to your own house now. I want to talk to your Mum and Dad. Charles and I are planning a boat adventure."

Chapter 17 - The Big Storm

For years Charles had been talking about making a sailing trip and wanting Alison to come with him. She would sail on the harbour with him, and she loved the exhilaration of beating to wind as it tossed back her hair and the boat heeled in the spray. But most of all she loved the simple joy it brought to Charles, the way his face flushed in the cool air and how that trademark wolfish grin, that she knew and loved so well, never left his face.

In 1885 Charles became an inaugural member of the Balmain Sailing Club. With his fast growing son, John, and with James when he visited, along with other local sailing friends, they would go flying across the harbour in an 18 foot open boat, going impossibly fast under huge canvass sails, often racing in the many regattas held on Sydney Harbour.

Sometimes Alison and the other children would join him in overnight trips on their own boat, named after them. These were mostly within the harbour but sometimes they sailed out of the harbour up the coast to the vast Hawkesbury River inlet or headed south to Botany Bay and Port Hacking. However they were rarely away for more than a couple days.

Alison had resisted Charles in his many previous entreaties to go and sail the wide ocean. Her reasons were many; work at the shop, children and grandchildren who all needed her. But now she knew it was time, time just for them, away and alone together, making the discovery of many new lands and horizons that were out there. Balmain had always held her so tight, and this hold would remain. But now she felt ready to go away, knowing that she could return to its fastness when needs must.

So today, having shared her secret with Sophie, she tripped along with a light heart to tell Maria and Jimmy of her plans. She was sure they would approve, in them lay a streak of the wild adventurers who had first come to this land. She arrived just as they were sitting down to a late lunch, and her enthusiasm was infectious. They all joined in the making of plans.

Charles' sister, Elizabeth, had established a farm over in New Zealand, more than 20 years ago, somewhere near Wellington. Elizabeth was now a grandmother to a brood of grandkids, most of whom Charles and Alison had never seen, and Elizabeth had written begging them to visit.

While they could have caught a steamer, Charles eyed off his little blue hulled boat, and so the plan was formed. Sophie had turned seven in the winter, and they would leave in the spring, when the winter storms were mostly past. With fine weather and fair wind a week would see them across the ocean and then, perhaps in autumn, they would return.

At last the day of the planned departure came. All Charles and Alison's children and grandchildren assembled. Many friends besides were there too It was a clear spring Saturday as they gathered for a picnic on the point at East Balmain. Charles and Alison shared an excited anticipation with all the well-wishers on warm sunny afternoon, as conversation and good spirits flowed. The boat was loaded, the sails were checked, they had provisions for a month and all was set. As the sun started to dip west a fair sea-breeze sprung up, as if a signal.

Charles stood up and stretched. It was time. So, with a small flotilla of following little boats and yachts, they were away. The others followed in their wake to Dawes Point then broke away. With a last wave they were ocean bound, heeled over into the breeze.

Four idyllic days of sailing followed, mostly light breezes and the odd heavy blow. But these were just scuds, and soon they sailed back into sun and fair weather again. They were more than half way there. Then, on the Thursday, far off to the south, they spied streamers and trailers of cloud. As the day passed they watched these grow, banking and piling, layer on layer into a huge lumpen mass, somewhere far out towards Tasmania. The sea took on a sullen unstructured shape and the wind died away until they were barely moving. It was almost soundless; a lone seagull squawk here and there, and creaking and flapping of loose sails as odd wind eddies passed.

Charles frowned; he knew the signs, tightened ropes and shortened the canvass. He and Alison went around the boat, checking to ensure everything was securely stowed.

Alison looked at him and his evident concern. She smiled brightly. "Don't worry, Charles, I know the signs out there. What will be, will be. Now we should eat and rest. It may be a long time until we can do so again."

So they prepared a simple meal and sat together in the stern, eating, with a sense of great contentment. Then they lay side by side in their bunk, held each other close and slept, her cheek resting on his chest and her hair in his face. A few times they almost woke, but feeling the comfort of the other, they snuggled close and slept again.

As the first rays of dawn were glowing in the east, their boat gave a shudder as the first gust of wind rocked it. They put on their oilskins and harnesses and went above.

Charles pointed the boat into the wind. He pulled in more sail; now just enough remained for steerage. Alison sat alongside him in the stern, they would wait and work together and, please God, they would make it home to Balmain to see their children again.

But she had no fear and no regrets. Her cup of life had been filled to overflowing with its gladness and sadness, and it had all been so good. And here they were now, still together.

An hour later the wind was howling and the waves were huge. The boat was driven before it, where they did not know, but towards the southeast. A day passed and a night. Their sails were torn and tattered, the main mast was split; it would break away soon. But they hung on and stayed together, driven down one wave before rising up over the crest of another in and endless cycle. Finally, as the second day faded, the sounds of wind and waves changed. Charles heard and knew the roar of breakers. He grabbed a sea anchor. But it was too late. So they held each other. A final peace washed over them, before a grinding roar as their boat piled and splintered on the rocks.

Next morning the storm had passed and a fisherman, near Greymouth, found splinters of broken timber on the beach. He headed further along to where the rocks loomed, black against the grey sea and sky. There he found them, a smashed boat with the name "Alison-Heather-Maria" painted in red on the stern and two bodies in oilskins, tied to their harnesses with arms locked around each other.

So Alison and Charles returned to Balmain, in a casket, but still together. They were laid beside the others in the little cemetery looking out to sea at the end of Balmain. Sophie and Maria cried at the grave, but another part of them was happy too, these people they loved so much were rejoined to their family, to be together always.

Chapter 18 - 1908 - Sophie and Matty

In June 1908 Sophie turned eight. Without her Gran her birthday seemed flat, but then she took her first Holy Communion. Her mother sewed for untold hours and hours to make her dress. It was pure white with fine white lace and brocade around the edges. And cleverly sewn across the top were the tiniest pale blue beads which sparkled in the light. After communion was over a man with a big flash camera took lots of photos of them all. Her father bought several, one for his mother and father, others for themselves. A small one in an oval frame was to go on the mantel in Sophie's room. She felt proud and very grown up.

Life was mostly good but she had taken to arguing over the silliest things with her Mum and neither could help themselves. Sophie had reached an age where she thought she knew almost everything about everything and, when she thought someone else said something she did not think was right, she could hardly help herself from saying so.

And, as well, her Mum was a little bit sad. She had tried to have another baby late last year, after they buried her Gran. But at the end of summer her waters broke and the baby was far too tiny to be born. So a melancholy had settled over her mother. It seemed she was often cross with Sophie over the smallest of things. Her Dad stayed patient and understanding and he tried to keep her Mum's spirits up, but she would get suddenly cross at him too, even when it was hard to see why. Sometimes that made Sophie really mad and so she would get cross with her Mum on account of her father, even though he always told Sophie not to interfere.

But the really good thing was Matty and her were best friends again. He had come up to her at her Gran's funeral and been so nice to her, as if to try and make up for the bad things he had said and done to her last year. Well not really bad, but a bit mean, like saying she was too little to join in with him and his friends. Just before Christmas he had come round again and brought her a beautiful little bird he had carved and painted. Sophie loved it so much and decided to bring it with her wherever she went. When Matty gave it to her he said to her he was sorry for being mean and nasty and it was a present to say he really liked her.

He also told her about his family and the bad things that were happening there. His father was drunk a lot and had started to hit his Mum more and more often when she screamed at him. And, just after New Year, he had gone to jail for two weeks for getting in a big fight when he was drunk; beating up another man who had to go to hospital. The magistrate said it was provoked because the other man had called him a 'useless drunk layabout', but, even so, he said he still had to send him a message about controlling his temper. The magistrate warned his father that if he did it again he would go to jail for much longer. Since then his Mum was often cross with Matty too, telling him to do more work to make up for his useless father, and screaming at him when he forgot things.

So, often, Matty and Sophie would go off together, just the two of them, and sit somewhere. They would talk and daydream about what they would do and the places they would go after they grew up; it was as if they both assumed that, whatever they did, they would do it together. Often, as they sat in these hidden places, along the cliffs where the heath bushes grew, they would see little birds with the bright blue markings, just like the one that Matty carved for her, flitting through the bushes. These became their symbol of happiness together. They always felt better when they saw one.

Sophie's other great treasure was the perfume bottle her Gran had given her. She often told it her happy stories and, with her mind, she gave it her memories to hold. At the moment it was mostly full of her doing happy things with Matty. Once, when she had found her Mum sitting in the corner crying, she had gone up and sat on her lap and taken one of her Mums tears and a few drops of her Mums perfume and put them both in the bottle together. Then she told her Mum that she loved her and wanted her to be happy again, and the bottle would help it happen.

Her Mum hugged and kissed her and said. "Oh Sophie, I love you all so much and I want to be happy too. But sometimes, when I think of my tiny little baby, too small to be born, I find myself crying and I sit in a chair all day unable to do anything. When your Dad comes home from a hard day's work, and is tired, I still have not washed the clothes or the plates, or cooked any dinner. Instead of complaining he sets to work and does it all himself. Then I find myself getting angry with him too, even though I know I am wrong."

Her Mum stood up, looked straight down at her daughter, and said, "It's funny, just saying it to you, and you with that funny little bottle to hold your secrets, makes me feel warm and happy. It makes it all easier to bear, at least for a little while."

About two months after her birthday Sophie woke, one morning, to hear her Mum screaming at her Dad. She rushed out and told her Mum to stop, then she shouted at her Mum that she was always cross and unfair.

Her Mum slapped her hard across the face. It was the first time she had hit her, ever. Sophie ran out of the house shouting "I hate you."

Her Dad tried to chase her but then went back to try and calm her Mum. Sophie waited down the road, crying quietly until the sting faded. She knew it would get better one day and when she went back home that night it would most likely be forgotten.

But for now she was mad as she could be, even though, deep down, she knew it was not really her Mum's fault. When the shouting stopped she went quietly back into her room, dressed quickly, packed her bag and, making sure she put her little blue bird in, left for school.

She was almost crying, but made herself hold it in as she walked down the street to meet Matty. They always walked to and from school together now. Matty had a face like thunder but he knew straight away she was upset too. So they sat on a step and she told him what had happened, and he told her the same for him, another fight with his Mum because of his Dad. They both felt better and walked up the street holding hands; truly they were best friends forever now.

At times during the day, in a daydream, the picture of her Gran and her sitting in that cave together came into her mind. She wasn't angry anymore. She remembered too that her Gran had said it was alright to show it to one special friend.

So, after school was finished, she came up to Matty with a cheeky grin and said. "I have a surprise I want to show you."

"What is it?" he said.

"It's a special surprise and I can only show it to one special friend. I want to show it to you."

She took his hand and led him down the path from school which went the opposite way from home. He cocked his head and looked puzzled at her. "Really, tell me what it is?"

She emphatically shook her head. "No, perhaps I will have to blindfold you, so you don't even know the way. You have to trust me."

They went on down the path, half way to her Gran's house, until Sophie found a side track into the bush. They followed this, mostly walking side by side and sometimes he had to follow her. As she came near the point where the cave was she could see someone had cleared some of the land on top. But the path led down the side, hidden below the cliffs and no-one could see them there. When she came to the part where they had to climb up the rocks she had to think a bit to remember clearly, but soon her mind had it right. There was the place, behind the bush behind that rock. She left Matty on the path and pushed into the bush until she saw the hole.

She decided she would quickly go inside and call Matty to see if he could find her. She called out, not too loud, "Matty."

"Where are you?" he said.

"You will have to find me," she called back.

For a minute there was the sound of scrabbling on the rocks. Suddenly, he was in there with her. "Wow, this is great," he said.

She unpacked her bag. As soon as she had this idea, earlier at school, she decided to save her lunch for this place; a sandwich, two biscuits and an apple. She tore the sandwich in half and passed Matty his half and a biscuit. "I brought a picnic to share," she said, feeling shy.

"Why thank you," he replied and doffed his hat with mock gallantry.

They both laughed. Sophie told him what her Gran had told her about her friend, Ruthie, the two of them coming here all those years ago, when her Gran was only about as old as she was now. She pointed, showing him the things left from way back then that were still here; the chest, the bottles, and other mementos. She opened the chest and took out the wooden bowl with the aboriginal patterns her Gran had shown her. She told him its story.

Matty nodded, "Amazing, it is hard to believe it is all so old. I think we should write Ruthie a message, in case she ever comes back to get it. We should say we would like to be her friends too."

So he took out his pen and a school book. He found a loose piece of paper which he wrote on, thanking Ruthie for letting them share this cave and telling the story of how they came to be here, had found the wooden bowl with her family's echidna totem, leaving it here for her to take back one day. He placed the note in the box and sat the bowl back in on top.

Sophie rummaged in her bag and found the blue bird he had given her, so like the blue wrens she saw in the garden. "I think I should leave this here too," she said. She placed it on top of the small chest. "It will be the mark of our special place."

Then she looked at Matty with her serious, serious eyes and said, "You must promise to never tell anyone else, not show this place to anyone else."

First he looked at her in a slightly amused, mocking way, as if to say, 'Don't be silly.' But the force in her eyes silenced him. He nodded, "I promise." He spat on his palm and rubbed it around, then held it to her and she joined her palm to his. It was a deal, stronger even than cross your heart.

Almost shyly he took her hand and put his arm around her shoulder. He gave her a half-hug, saying. "I like you so much Sophie. I am glad you showed me. When our parents are mean to us, we can come here together and no one else will know."

She nodded wisely, "It's a deal."

***

Up above two men, Joe and Fred, were working. Their job was to build a tank on the headland. Below would be a jetty where the ships would come to pump out oil into the tank. This oil would be used for other ships and for the new cars that were coming to the streets.

But first they had to get the top land level so the tank could sit flat. There were some big rocks, too big for their crowbars to lift. They unpacked sticks of dynamite to use to move the large rocks. The plan was to set the explosive sticks down into gaps alongside the rocks until they were buried below the ground and use the explosions to break up or move these rocks.

They started next to a big rock close to the edge, pushing an explosive stick down each side of it into gaps between it and the dirt. As they worked, once or twice they thought they heard a faint voice, like a child.

"Did you hear that?" said Joe to Fred.

"Maybe," Fred replied. He looked over the side. Nothing was there. He looked again then shrugged.

"Must have been a bird," he said to Joe.

They ran out the fuse, across to the far side of the clearing where the ground fell away. Joe lit the two fuses and for a few seconds they watched the fire flare and snake across the top. Then, as it got close, they ducked down the side, behind the rock shoulder. There was a dull thump as the first charge went off. A few seconds later came another thump as the second charge followed. The rock cracked and dropped below the ground surface.

Fred said, "That's good. We can level off the ground without moving that rock now."

So they shovelled loose dirt into the hole until it was full and used a rake to level the ground so no one would ever know there had been anything here. Then they moved on to lay the next charge."

***

Below Sophie and Matty paused for a second in their serious talking. Suddenly there was a loud crashing thud and some of the roof came down next to them.

Matty grabbed her hand and pulled Sophie towards him. After a moment of hesitation he said. "We must go, get out of here". They moved towards the entrance.

There was a second bang, but they barely knew, as the whole roof crashed down on them.

Sophie felt an instant of fright as she saw the roof coming. Then there was a sudden extra bright white light. She and Matty pulled out of their bodies and rose above the cave, still holding hands.

She could see her Gran smiling and beckoning to her. She brought Matty with her, across to her Gran. Her Gran wrapped them both tight in her arms.

Chapter 19 – Where has Sophie Gone?

Maria was working in the kitchen peeling vegetables for dinner. An image of Sophie's face flashed before her, coming with a jolt, followed by a fragment of a glimpse of Sophie and Matty, hands linked. Standing near but apart, watching on, was her Mum, Alison. It was as if they were all in another place. Then the picture was gone. All at once she felt empty and very scared.

She sensed something was missing from the thread of invisible connection to her daughter. It had always lived deep down inside her; now it felt like it had been torn away. She shivered and decided to block the thought out. She worked away for a while, finishing preparing the dinner before she looked at the clock. Sophie really should be home soon, it was getting late. She really wanted to give her a big hug and tell her she was sorry about this morning. She hated what she had done and knew this was the limit; she must pull herself together, stop moping around and getting angry for no reason.

She went out to the front verandah. Alexander was playing there with Rachel. "Alex, did Sophie come home with you?"

He shook his head. "She always walks with Matty now. But I saw them together just after school finished. They were standing and talking near the gate. Then I started home with my friends."

Another half hour passed. The sun was falling below the horizon, on which sat a huge bank of clouds as if a storm was coming. Surely they should be home by now. Deep fear gripped her, a superstitious dread.

She decided she would walk down to the McNeil house. Perhaps they had gone there first and forgotten the time. But Mrs McNeil said she had not seen them either, She thought Matty must have stopped behind with Sophie, at her house, for a while.

Then Mrs McNeil turned to Maria and said. "I have this bad feeling. I so wanted to say sorry to Matt for being cross this morning. It's Dan you know, too much drink and a temper. So I push things onto Matty and I get cross when he can't do it all or forgets. He is a good boy, really. An hour ago I suddenly see his face and then it's gone. Now I have this scared feeling, sick in the pit of my stomach with dread."

Maria nodded, "Me too!"

Their fear was palpable. They both walked up to Maria's house. When they were almost at the gate, Maria saw Jimmy walking towards her along the footpath. She felt a second of relief; he would know what to do. He was always so practical. But the dread hit her again, like walking into a wall. Jimmy knew, before he reached her, that something was badly wrong.

Quickly she told him what she knew; how Sophie and Matty had not come home, even though it was almost dark. Mrs McNeil added in her bit. Maria did not say anything about the bad feeling, desperate not to let it into her mind, but as she spoke there was an ominous rumble of a storm coming which mirrored the turmoil within.

"Right, well we must go and find them, a storm is coming and we don't want them caught in it," Jimmy said. "Perhaps they got lost or one has fallen and is hurt. They are always going off traipsing together.

"Let's take our children to Betty, across the way, and ask her to mind them. Then I will go to the West End Hotel and ask the men I know there to come and help us look. In the meantime you can start knocking at the doors of the neighbours along the street to ask if anyone has seen them."

Three hours of fruitless searching followed, first with the men from the hotel, then with the police and all the other neighbours. It was not helped by the rain which came streaming down, wetting them all, washing away tracks and leaving the ground wet and slippery.

The only thing that anyone knew was that a couple of children from the school had seen Sophie and Matt going off together, walking along the path, the opposite way from home. The search party door knocked all the people who lived near the school that way. One person had seen the two children walking together, along the road past their house, about a hundred yards from the school but, after that, nothing.

Finally, late in the night, a policeman brought them back to their home. "You must collect your children and rest now. We can do no more tonight. In the morning I have organised for over a hundred men to help us search, once it is light enough to see."

Jimmy and Maria collected their two small ones and brought them home to bed. Then they sat, side by side but not touching. Finally Maria reached out to him, took his hand and gave a big shuddering sob. "If only I had not slapped her and shouted at her this morning. I so wanted to see her this afternoon and say sorry and tell her I would never do it again. But now I am so scared I will not have the chance."

She told Jimmy about her awful premonition that afternoon. He sat in silence and looked at her. As she spoke she watched his face. It was as if all the light went out in his eyes. He really, totally, believed her premonitions; remembering finding her crying on that day when her mother's boat hit the rocks. It was days later before news of the storm and wreck came.

He sobbed and put his face in his hands. "Oh, not my Sophie. Please let it not be true."

But, although he knew neither how nor what had happened, in his heart of hearts he knew it was so. His dearest little girl, with the big bright eyes and shining dark hair, was forever gone from him. How he ached to hold her and see her smile, but yet he knew it would not happen again. He cried until he could cry no more. Maria held him, trying to feed him her strength, and give him back the comfort he had so often given her. Her heart ached so much, but his need and grief were stronger.

Finally he stood up, a grim look on his face, saying, "Still we must find her, even if it is so."

In the morning the police and neighbours offered words of hope and comfort and he pretended to believe. One hundred and fifty men scoured every place where they thought they might find them, around the shores, in the gullies, on the hilltops, around all the wharfs and vacant lots, but nothing. They said they would check the bars, interview and ask questions of sailors and anyone who might know, but still nothing. So they checked for all the ships that might sail or were just gone, nothing again.

Jimmy could not bring himself to join in all of this other inquiry. For him all that mattered was to find his little girl, even if only to discover her broken body. So he searched and he searched; he searched in sunshine, he searched in rain, crisscrossing the peninsula and all the other places nearby, rowing along the shores, using his dog to search for scent. But there was no trace, nothing, nothing, nothing.

His soul raged at the emptiness. But still he continued, gone before dawn and returning far into the night to fall into a restless sleep of exhaustion. Two months had passed with still nothing. His will was broken. He could search no more. Now he sat silently, alone in the chair in her room, and stared. He did not talk to Maria, other than a grunt. He barely talked to the children; even when they came up to him and tried to tell him things, their special stories of the day, he only half looked. His eyes were somewhere else. After a minute or two they would walk away, looking crestfallen.

From the first day Maria and Mrs McNeil told police of the arguments of the morning; not that they themselves believed this was more than a passing flash. But it was the only thing left for others to believe. It became the story; that the children had run away, to who knows where. So they all waited, with a small and diminishing hope. Departed ships came to next ports, telegraphs were sent ahead, all leads were checked, but nothing, nothing, nothing!

Finally Rosie and Michael talked to the priests at their church and to Maria's brother and sister and to Mrs McNeil who went to the Presbyterian Church. It was agreed, they must all pray, if not for their safe return, at least for the safe passage of their children's souls.

So, on an early summer's day, the two congregations gathered. For an hour they sat, as one, in prayerful silence. Their priests, standing together, led them in prayer for their two beloved children.

Then they all said their communions and sang a hymn of praise to their Gods for his deliverance of these two children.

It was the only time anyone could remember a joining of the churches. They all sat together, in the big new Catholic Church, alongside the school to which the children had gone, with the steeple of the Presbyterian Church to their side and its bells ringing to call them all to prayer. When it was over people stood outside for hours; whispering words of hope and comfort. In their common anguish they came together as never before.

Jimmy had sat beside Maria in the church, alone together at the front. Their children were with his parents behind them. Mrs McNeil sat with her family, together at the other side.

Jimmy could cry no more, and he could feel no goodness in the prayer. But other hope was gone, so he sat there with a numb empty mind, drawing a small comfort from all these people and their care. He remembered how they had greeted him in the streets as he walked with Maria, a small Sophie holding his hand. Then, of the days and nights when these many good people had helped, searching for his daughter and the boy.

He saw the children in his mind now, as he had last seen them on that day; two small children walking past his house together, holding hands and deep in conversation as they made their way to school. He knew, since that day, with an absolute certainty, that they did not run off together.

Maria dabbed her eyes and tried to draw her God to her, and reach out her soul to him. She grieved greatly for her lost daughter, but even more she grieved for the hurt and broken man beside her; her husband and the rock of her life these past nine years; but now so lost, so desolate. Now she must try to heal him as he had helped to heal her all those years before.

When the service was done the others got up to leave. Jimmy went with them; he could sit no longer still in the silence. He had to do something, but he knew not what. So he walked and kept walking. That night, when he fell to the ground asleep, he found himself in a place far from all he knew. The next day still he walked. As he walked blueish mountains rose in the distance, he felt they were drawing him towards them

Maria stayed still, sitting in the church, long after the others were gone, and let the silence enfold her. At last, in the faded light she felt the whisper of her daughter's breath and the music of her laughter. She saw Sophie now, walking hand in hand with Matty, along with her mother and a small dark girl. With this vision came understanding that, for them, all was well. But for her, she must go on; to tend to her family and give hope to the living.

She went home and sat in Sophie's room, just herself, her daughter's invisible presence wrapped around her. She picked up Sophie's framed communion picture, carried it back to church, found the priest and asked him bless it and say a prayer over it, as a mass card for the safe passage of her daughter's soul.

She returned to her home, still alone, and picked up Sophie's treasured blue and silver perfume bottle and held it. She breathed in Sophie's scent and warmth one last time. For a minute she thought that, perhaps, this bottle should pass to Rachel for it to continue with her family. But she knew the link was broken. It had to pass on to another life in another time.

So she reached into the fireplace and placed the bottle and picture, side by side on a small ledge, as high up as she could reach. Perhaps they would end in a flaming fire, or perhaps, in a time yet to be imagined, they would be found again, and the image and memory of her daughter could live again.

She closed the door of her daughter's room and walked again to the church to bring home Alexander and Rachel, waiting with their dear Gran Rosie. Of Jimmy there was no sign. She walked home with Mrs McNeil and told her of her vision. Mrs McNeil seemed comforted.

A month passed and still there was no Jimmy, then two, then six, then twelve months were gone. Maria forced herself to continue with her life, getting up each day, taking her children to school, working at the shop, calling to Mrs McNeil. But sometimes, deep in the night, she felt as if the loneliness and pain would overwhelm her.

Her strongest comfort was the help of Jimmy's friends. Those rough men of the docks and pubs gave her more kindness than anyone else she knew. At least once a week a couple of them would call, often with cakes from their wives or other gifts that they bought, things she knew they could ill afford. There were presents for her children, repairs for the house and, at odd times, just a word of encouragement. She remembered back to those long days and nights when they had helped Jimmy maintain the search. Long after all hope was gone, one or two would row with Jimmy around the headlands, or would stumble alongside him across the hills and gullies, not believing, no longer hoping, but helping anyway.

Her second treasure was her children, though it grieved her to see them made adults before their time. Alexander was always the first to help, to do the extra jobs. Rachel, who she now understood had a great place of pain inside her too with Sophie gone, would come to her bed sometimes in the small hours, when she felt as if her own world was falling in, to hug and hold her. Together, in these darkest hours, they would rebuild their strength.

She knew too she had to continue to bring light to her children's lives. So she taught them to sing songs she knew. They would sing together as they worked, joining voices and choruses. In these moments a strange ethereal bond of joy arose from their music.

Finally, as it came around toward the end of the second year, the day before it would have been Sophie's birthday of ten years, with her children much grown, and with her singing with them as she worked away out the back, Maria heard the front gate swing.

Jimmy stood in the door and listened. It was the singing that he knew so well and at once there was lightness in his soul. She waited for him yet! There she stood, her light undimmed, her hair flaming in the afternoon sun. She turned and smiled, unsure. A stranger stood before her, hair gone gray, back bent from toil. And yet it was him. Her heart sang so loud to burst. She opened her arms. After a long time, so still, holding together, bodies touching like gossamer, they talked, first to their children and then, at last, to each other.

He told her of his travels and of the empty years, and how, only in the sunsets, looking far across the empty horizons, could he find some solace for his soul. How he worked out there shearing sheep, from dawn till dark and until his back could barely straighten. How he got up one day and knew she again had great need of him and how he must be there again for his wife and his children. Then of being driven to cross the miles and miles to reach her before she would sit alone on Sophie's next birthday, with the slow tears of loneliness rolling down her cheeks. His mind had seen that picture of her so clearly and he could not bear for it to be.

She told him of the children and his parents, and then of her vision of Sophie with her own mother and her knowledge of it being well for them.

Jimmy knew she told the truth, that her heart did not lie. He felt the lifting of a weight. She told him of her loneliness without him and her need for him, that often she lay in bed in the small hours and longed so much to hear his voice and feel his touch. Sometimes in her half sleep she would reach out for him only to find the empty place where he should have been.

It was truly good that they were together again; two broken parts, re-joined and made whole.

Next day they walked to the point at East Balmain and stood next to the graves, so many lives. There Maria told Jimmy how her sister had moved to live in a big house across the water in Sydney town and that her brother, who had taken Tom and Mary's house when her parents died, had now gone to London to live with his English wife.

So now both houses lay empty and she did not know what to do with them. She could sell them if she chose but they were too dear to her.

Soon it was agreed. Tom and Mary's house would be theirs. The other two they would rent and, when their children were grown, if they had need of them they would be theirs. For themselves, they wanted to live in the big sandstone house with the view, where they had first truly met. They also wanted it again to be a house full of children and laughter; those they had already and, with luck, more yet to come, a whole tribe please God.

In three more years three more children came and they knew it was enough. On quiet summer nights they would walk down to the beach, and sit staring out across the harbour, watching as stars rose in the east, sitting on the rock where they first had made their promises to each other. The first war came and went and all their children lived still. When their daughter Rachel was grown she moved to the house across the way, the first Balmain house, Roisin. Soon she had children and they had grandchildren, and again they thrilled to the patter of small feet.

The hard years of the Depression came. Now there was barely money to buy food and customers stayed away from their shop of exquisite things. But Jimmy, ever resourceful, found new ways for them to live. He bought and sold furniture, often broken and needing repair, but sold for a pittance as families were forced out of houses and could not take it with them. With skill and care and his masterful hands, he would fix the locks and hinges, polish the wood, fix the legs. When he was finished it was as good as new; and those with the money would desire it. So their lives continued.

The house in Smith St now had McNeil's living in it. First they rented it to Mrs McNeil's second son Robert and his new wife. Robert was young, hard-working and with the manner and looks of Matty. Then Dan McNeil died in a pub brawl. Ruth McNeil had worked hard all her life. Now she was old and tired. She found Dan had almost drunk their family house away.

When her house was sold and the debts were paid Ruth McNeil had barely a pittance remaining. Robert was determined his mother would come and stay with him, even though he had two small children of his own.

Jimmy and Maria knew help was required. So they determined their precious house, 'Casa Ardwyn', in Smith St, should go to Robert.

He was so like Matty, the son in law they might have had. They found a way he could afford it that did not seem like charity. So now the title deeds were his. They knew Sophie would be well pleased.

As the years rolled on Robert's family grew up and Mrs McNeil died. The house was sold again, forgotten whose first it had been. Still the new owners clearly loved it and cared for it. Sometimes Maria and Jimmy walked along Smith St and came past it. In the front they would stop and admire the pretty roses and daises in the garden. Most years they walked past in the summer, when the frangipani tree was in bloom, stopping to smell its fragrance. Sometimes Jimmy would pick a flower and place it in Maria's hair. Just rarely they would see a person there, glimpsed through the window.

One day, as they came by, a little boy came out pushing a red tricycle, perhaps a year of two younger than their Sophie had been. They smiled at him. He smiled back, a happy boy with his toy.

They did not say anything but, in his place, they saw the image of their lost child on her red tricycle. It tore into their hearts opening the pain anew. After that they did not come again.

Chapter 20 - 1942 – Discovery

The year was 1942. Sydney was under attack, with a Japanese submarine found in the harbour. There were army and navy people everywhere. Ships needed fuel and fuel needed tanks. The navy looked for good safe places to build tanks, not too close to where anyone lived in case of bombs, but on deep water where the big ships could come and go.

One such place was Ballast Point, where a single big oil tank stood, used for the diesel fuel for truck and ship engines for more than 30 years, but now, leaking an oily film at the seams. The Navy decided this old tank was no longer safe and must come out. Into its place would go three brand new, larger and stronger, steel tanks. So the fitters cut apart the old tank's iron plates and lifted off the metal base plate with a ship's crane.

Below the old tank was sandstone rock mixed with sand and rubble, sitting over bedrock. It needed to be excavated further for the bigger, stronger, foundations. So they brought in their machines; dozers, trenchers, backhoes, and cranes, to scrape away the soil and move the loose rock and then lift off the heavy pieces until they were on solid bedrock onto which they would lay a new cement foundation.

There was one big rock slab at the front, closest to the sea, tipped at a strange angle, as if it had been dropped crookedly before. Part of it poked up above the ground. This needed to be lifted away to finish the levelling. They brought in their heaviest crane, and secured the cable around this large boulder. With a grinding of gears the crane took up the strain and slowly the heavy rock was raised out of its hole and swung aside.

A dozer rolled forward to push aside the earth and remove the cavity. As it rumbled into place a worker standing to the side let out a whistle.

He raised a hand and gave a shout to signal "Stop".

Everyone paused. He waved the other onlookers to come over and look for themselves. In this hole were a couple bottles and something else, white things. They lay in pieces on the ground. He climbed down. He realised he was looking at a human skeleton, not an adult but a child, in fact two children. Some long bones were broken as were the skulls, as if crushed by a heavy weight.

"We should call the Military Police," said the site foreman.

They waited for an hour and two Military Policemen arrived.

"Whoever it was has been dead for a long time, and you need to get on with your work," said the first MP.

So the MPs collected the remains and the other things from the hole.

One wrote a short report in his notebook for logging at the base.

In it he listed the items. "One green bottle, one blue bottle, one small chest, one blue carved bird, knife, bell, remains of some clothes and bags, maybe some bits of books," he wrote.

He continued, "Remains appear to be two children, likely age between 6 and 12, perhaps a boy and girl, don't appear aboriginal."

Once all was collected they put the objects into bags with labels, then drove away to lodge the remains with the civilian police. In due course a police officer, Constable Jones, lodged them, along with the original report, with the coroner.

Many people were dying at this time and the coroner's staff was down to one; the others had been co-opted for the war effort. So the coroner glanced briefly at the bags' contents. He made an entry into his log and his assistant collected the human remains along with the other detritus and put them, along with the original report, into a box which he labelled with the date and record number. He placed this into a storage compartment and closed the door, his work done. Perhaps, one day, when time permitted, someone would examine these items properly.

As the war progressed, the deposition of more body remains continued, but, except in major finds or obvious homicides, the investigation was kept to a minimum. So they accumulated, each lot tagged, lodged in its container and placed into storage. When the war ended they were all moved together, into a new storage place, unopened. There they stayed.

Slowly their existence and provenance drifted out of human memory.

With the war and all its comings and goings in Sydney Harbour there was no longer room for a small neglected cemetery, at the foot of the hill, near the ferry wharf at Balmain. The gravestones were old and overgrown. They seemed to have been forgotten. Another cemetery in Leichardt had become the place of burials for many years.

One day, with no permission sought from people who lived nearby or from known relatives, a team of workers arrived. By the end of three days the graves were all removed. They were placed together in a group in Leichardt. A small sign was left behind to advise anyone who cared about the removal. No one seemed to notice and no disrespect was intended, but it was wartime and things needed to be done.

Chapter 21 - Rachel remembers

Rachel felt old and tired. This morning, with the cold in the stone house, she had found it hard to get out of bed and her arthritis pained her. Still, after almost her allotted four score years, she still found simple pleasures in life. But today she felt troubled. It was hard to think exactly why that should be; perhaps it was just the passage of time, so much change over so many years.

When she had first come to this house, so very long ago, it was like a light had been turned on in her life. Seen through her six year old eyes this house seemed huge after their small Balmain cottage. She had never been back there since, she could not say why. Even though she knew she had been happy there, that leaving closed a dark chapter of her life.

But now she must remember. She drew her mind back to that time. An image of Sophie came floating into her mind, in her white communion dress, like in the picture her Mum had given her, when she was old and dying. Now she remembered that day. As she remembered she understood why she was troubled and what she must do. It was getting hard to remember sometimes, but today she would make herself remember. It needed to be today! If she left it until tomorrow perhaps her mind would be unable to hold it any more.

She knew her memory was not good; sometimes she did not know where she was or what she was doing; sometimes a kindly neighbour had to help her find her way home. The doctor called it something with a funny long name that started with an O sound, Ozzimers, or something like that.

Her one son lived far away in that City called New York. His job was something to do with money, Investment Banker; that was it. He decided, three months ago when he heard she was getting lost, that someone must stay in the house to help her. Now a lady lived with her called Maggie. She was nice, but she was a bit of a bother to always have around.

But what did that matter, she knew what was wrong, she was old. All her friends had gone and, before long, she would join them. She was nearly ready to cross over, that's what she thought it was like ever since her dear mother, Maria, had told her the full story. But, before she did, she must first tell her daughter about her mother's, her grandmother's and her own stories, She must do it to keep the memory alive, in case someone ever found where Sophie had gone.

That was what she had been trying hard to remember, keeping alive this memory for Sophie. She had woken last night knowing that she could still just hold the story in her mind, in order to tell it. But it must be today or it may be too late. She pulled into her mind and held tight to what her mother, Maria, had told her a few days before she died. At that time it had been troubling her mother's soul, this need to not let the missing Sophie be completely forgotten, to ensure that her story be passed on lest anyone ever discover what had come of her.

She remembered too the pain that would come into her father's eyes whenever Sophie's name came up. It was, as her mother said, "harder to have one vanish and never know the where or why, than to see them die."

So, while her mother and father got on with life, after Sophie, creating a new happy family, the hole of her absence was always there. And if Rachel was truthful it had been like that for her too, she kept a lock on images of Sophie, blocking them from her mind. Mostly it had worked, but not quite. Now it was time to let them come back, to recall and tell another.

She made a cup of tea and a slice of buttered toast. Sitting at the old wooden kitchen table, she felt those remembrances of her earliest childhood swirl around in her mind and rise to the surface.

The strongest was of sitting on the bed with Sophie, in their room with the pink fireplace. Perhaps she was three. Sophie must have been in her second year of school because she was beginning to read, mostly picture books with a few words on each page. But Sophie and Rachel both thought Sophie was enormously clever. Even more than the reading Rachel loved the pictures and, while she could look at the pictures by herself, Sophie's reading brought them alive in her mind. Perhaps that was why she had loved painting herself; it had been her own effort to recreate those early pictures that had flowed through her mind. Her daughter, Sarah, shared her love of painting too. Sarah had gone on to do it so much better than she, Rachel, ever could.

Sophie's favourite books were those about faraway lands, places with pictures of ships to take you there, travelling over vast blue seas. Lands of amazing high mountains with snow and pictures of waterfalls; and pictures of astonishing animals, the giraffes with their long necks, zebras that looked like funny painted horses, jaguars with their orange and black mottled skins that swam in the water and climbed in trees and huge brightly coloured parrots that flew overhead in the forests.

She remembered how, sometimes, Sophie would get so interested in the stories that she would read on and on, page after page, turning too fast, before Rachel could look properly at the pictures. When this went on for long she would eventually get bored and fall off to sleep. Sometimes she just pretended to go to sleep, to get Sophie to stop reading and tuck her into bed, with a big hug and kiss, pretending to be Mummy or Daddy.

Rachel also remembered her Gran Alison and, sort of, Grandpa Charles. But that memory was all smoky in her head, like you pushed your face up against frosted glass and tried to look through, but all you could really see were half shadowed outlines. There was something special between Sophie and Gran; it was like they could talk to each other without looking or saying anything. Rachel really liked her Gran, she made you feel warm inside, like you were the most important person there was.

She remembered too the first time Sophie showed her the beautiful perfume bottle that her Gran had given her, covered in silver flowing waves, washing over a smoky, almost milky, turquoise sea of glass. All at once Rachel had felt so jealous. *Why did Grandma give it to Sophie, not me?*

This feeling flooded back now, she felt the raw anger of her child mind rise again and then she recalled that day, long ago, when she decided to pay Sophie back for being chosen to have this thing.

When Sophie went out with her Mum and Alexander, leaving only her and her Dad at home, Rachel had taken the perfume bottle and hidden it away in the back of the fireplace, high on a little ledge. After Sophie came back Rachel had watched her carefully. She was expecting Sophie to look for the perfume bottle where she last left it, or perhaps look in other places when she did not find it, then to ask if Rachel knew where it was.

Rachel had made up her mind to deny knowledge of where the perfume bottle was gone. Instead she would wait until Sophie was not there to take it out and play with it, all by herself. If Sophie caught her with it she would tell her she had found it, fallen under the rug and was minding it.

But Sophie had not done that. Instead of asking Rachel or searching for it she stood in the middle of the room looking puzzled for a few seconds. Then she walked over to the fireplace, reached up for the bottle and took it out. Sophie did not scold Rachel, it was as if she did not think Rachel had hidden if, but it had moved there by itself. All Sophie said was. "There you are, you naughty little bottle, you know you can't hide from me."

Next day Sophie said to her, "The bottle wants to be shared between us, so you must also use it to hold your memories." So, after that, they would sit together, each putting in their memories, side by side on the bed. Sophie now called it 'our perfume bottle', which really meant they both owned it.

Another thing about Sophie that Rachel remembered clearly was the day, when her Grandma and Grandpa had died; it was a long time before other people found out about it. She and Sophie were talking about boys, or mainly Sophie was talking about Matty, in that 'I love you' way she had. Rachel was saying she thought boys were silly, feeling grown up talking like that with her sister. Suddenly Grandma was with them in their house, not on the boat which had crashed.

Rachel knew straightaway that Sophie felt it, and she knew her Mummy felt it too, even though Mummy was outside the room. It seemed like a hole was open that let her Grandma in with them and let them see out into another place where the broken boat was.

That memory drifted away. Then pain rose into Rachel's mind. It was now the day Sophie had gone away and not come back. She heard her mother asking Alexander where Sophie was. Then her Mum went down the street to look for her at the McNeil's. While she was gone there Rachel took out the perfume bottle. There was a big flash of lightning as she did this. It frightened her. And the bottle felt like horrible, like ice. It was cold and empty, with nothing inside. It hurt her hand to hold it. After that she left it in the bedside locker and did not take it out again. Then, from the day of the big church service the bottle was gone. Rachel knew at once where her mother put it, up in the chimney, but she did not want to touch it again.

When Sophie went away her Mummy and Daddy did not understand she missed Sophie just as much as they did. They thought because she was only four she would soon forget her. But she could not forget, and sometimes she felt really sad and most wanted Sophie to come back, and sometimes she felt really angry because it was mean of Sophie to go away too soon.

She remembered wanting to talk to her Daddy, soon after Sophie went away. But it was like he could not see her, even though she could see him. So she took his hand and said his name to make him look at her. For a second he saw her then his eyes went away to somewhere inside his head and she felt so hurt because she knew he had forgotten she was there. After that she did not try to talk to him anymore, and she tried her best not to think of Sophie either.

Later she remembered that awful time when her Daddy was away for ages and ages, and her Mum had tried so hard to be brave and worked so hard. All her bad, angry part, from before Sophie went away, was gone; the times like when she sat in the chair and cried and argued with her Dad; now Rachel understood that was about the two little babies that died. But once her Daddy went away, even though she never got cross anymore, sometimes her Mummy would get so tired and lonely. And sometimes, at night, Mummy would cry in her sleep. Then Rachel would go in to her and cuddle close and they would both help each other to forget their sadness. Then, by helping her Mummy, Rachel started to feel better too.

The final memory from that time, and a happy one, was when Mummy had decided to teach her and Alexander to sing as they all worked together. Mostly her Mum sung the verses and they sung the chorus, but sometimes they had sung all together. One day they were learning a new harmony and her Mum said, "We all have to try really hard to make this beautiful, because then Daddy will hear this in his heart, no matter how far away he is, and it will bring him back. And it had!

Suddenly Rachel awoke from her reverie. She must have sat there, lost in remembering, for over half an hour because now her tea was cold.

She rang the bell and Maggie came, that's what she called her, though Margaret was her proper name. "I need to go across and see Sarah. Would you ring her, to make sure she is in, and then take me over. You needn't stay but perhaps you could come again to help me home after lunch."

As she got up to leave, all those old memories from Smith Street came back again, with a clarity that almost took her breath away, all flooding into her mind together. Today was their day, they must all be told.

She shook her head to clear it then went to the dresser drawer to take out a small bunch of old photos and letters. These would help prompt her memory, so little to show for 80 years of living and all that had passed. But it was what she had and it would have to do.

Maggie offered to drive her in the car, but no, she would prefer to walk. It gave her time to collect her thoughts and hold them all together in one place before the wind blew them away, like sheets of paper caught in a wind gust, scattered all over the ground. Together they made a coherent whole, but each piece of paper by itself meant so little. As she walked more and more memories of other times came flooding back.

There, across the harbour, was Millers Point, where a windmill had once stood. Now a huge ocean liner stood in front of it and behind it rose all the skyscrapers of the city. They said that they had built one that was over fifty stories tall, imagine that!

Out on the harbour a grand sail boat came sweeping past. That brought to mind her days of sailing with her Dad, and then with her beloved David, both long gone. How she had loved those times, wind in her face and her hair blowing out behind, 'like a golden cloud', her David said. If he could only see it now, so grey and thin.

The only pity of it was that Maria would not sail with them, she never said why, but smiled brightly when asked and said, "I leave that for others." Perhaps it had to do with when the news came of that terrible storm and of Granny and Grandpa with their boat broken on the rocks. Rachel could just remember how a man came to the door with a telegram. Even though her Mum felt it before, then it was in writing, like being hit in the face.

Her Mum had taken the telegram with a shaking hand and passed it to her Dad, then stood in the passage and cried. Her Dad put his arms around her Mum and said soft words. Rachel had come up to them and asked them what was the matter?

Her Dad had pulled her in against them and said. "This is saying that Grandma and Grandpa are dead and the boat is wrecked. We are all very sad. So now we must hold a happy memory of them." After she hadn't really been sad because she knew they were somewhere good together.

She felt flooding into her mind a picture of Gran Alison and Grandpa Charles, young and beautiful on their wedding day, perhaps it was an old photograph, but where did the colour and that red gold light in her Gran's hair come from? She could only remember her with soft gray hair. They did not take coloured pictures at her Gran's wedding, just funny old black and white things. But still it was a real picture, she knew it was.

It came to her as almost an afterthought. All at once she wished Gran had outlived Sophie, they were like shared souls. If anyone knew where to look for Sophie it would have been her Gran. *Oh, if only she could know too!*

She had arrived, she was standing at the front gate of the little cottage, still with all the beautiful roses, some were there from long before, some she had planted, and now some more that Sarah had planted.

Her daughter was an artiste; that was how she called it. She painted beautiful pictures of the city and harbour and of the old houses and people of Balmain. She sold them at the Balmain and Rozelle markets. That brought to mind her own pictures of the harbour bridge. The bridge was not there when she was little but she remembered them building it in the bad years of the Depression and how a man she knew from Millers Point had fallen off and died. She had done a series of pictures to tell that story, beginning with its unoccupied space. She had watched it grow from the two ends as she walked home with her children from Nicholson St School,

Pity Sarah had no children; she missed sounds of their feet and chatter in a house. Then she thought, *Sarah's children would be grown up by now*, but then, perhaps, they would have had some children of their own.

Right now she must stop her thinking from rambling away and hold her thoughts together for one last time as she told her daughter the story.

Her daughter, Sarah, welcomed her with a happy smile and kiss on the cheek. Rachel realised that she was a pretty one, even the other side of fifty, though her hair was a bit too red, it must be that extra bottle colour, and her breasts were sagging. *That's what comes of not wearing a bra.*

She said "Dearest, I have come to tell you a story before it is too late." She handed Sarah the letters and photos and said, "I have brought these. You must use them to help me remember, if I get muddled."

They sat in front of the fire, two chairs side by side, with the photos on her lap as she told it; the story that needed to be said, some from her own remembering and some as told by Maria on that last day.

When she had finished Sarah offered her tea, but Rachel said "No, walk me home please. I am finished all I set out to do. Pray God it is enough."

As she walked home she felt Sophie smiling at her, saying "Thank you my little sister. Soon, together, we will see the pictures of our childhood again, but they will be completely real this time."

Then her thoughts turned to this house to which she came; they were such wonderful thoughts; such happy thoughts. How, a week after her Dad had returned, they had come here and it seemed like a fairy castle.

On the day they left the other house she had taken out the perfume bottle, from where her Mum had hidden it, for one last time to say goodbye. It was warm again and she knew that Sophie was safe with Gran Alison. But still there had been pain and missing when she thought of her sister. She had spent her whole life until today trying to block it out. At last no more!

More thoughts flowed of her Dad and Mum and all five of them, children in the house, playing and singing together and sailing, then of her David and her with baby Sarah and of three year old Tom holding Sarah so proudly. It was good and it was enough.

Two days later Maggie rang Sarah. She said Rachel had died in her sleep. She seemed to be smiling and was holding two pictures. One was of her and David on a boat, the other of a family outside a different house, which had written on the back, 'Sophie's 5th birthday 1905'.

Chapter 22 - Sarah

Sarah had never felt the passage of time until that day her mother had come to visit and told her the story of her family. Now her need to pass this story on vexed her and made her feel anxious. It had been there since that day but had not diminished over time, not even after she painted the story which that day had given her. Instead, year on year it grew inexorably stronger as she felt the sands of her life slipping through rheumy fingers.

She always thought she would have children of her own, but somehow it had never happened. Perhaps, if she had found that special man; maybe then it would have been something that they both got organised about and made occur, a love child. Now that time had passed.

She remembered with fondness some men in her life, happy memories; wild, funny, joyous, passionate memories. There were parts where she was a bit too stoned to remember clearly, a psychedelic blur. While not a child of the sixties she was definitely a young woman of that era and had enjoyed the artistic liberation along with all the others.

What parties they had in this house, often there were half a dozen of them as loosely arranged couples, with their own bedrooms for some intimate coupling when wanted, but mostly sitting around in the living room, sprawled on bean bags, rugs and half broken chairs, discussing art, politics and how they would save the world.

Her art had been the one abiding passion of her life. It had come from her Mum, a love of pictures and paintings, not that she had understood the place it had first come from until her Mum had at the very last told her about little Sophie, of her reading stories to Rachel as a child. Now she understood the source, it was her own legacy from Sophie. It took the form of a burning desire to capture images as they flowed through her mind, create them and bring them alive on canvass.

She had wonderful memories, a child in the garden with her mother, paint and easel set up. Rachel painted, often laboriously, capturing images that passed before her eyes, boats sweeping across the harbour, dawn lit silhouettes of the city, the sky, perfect flowers that grew in spring and that series of amazing pictures of the making of the Sydney Harbour Bridge.

Before long she started helping her mother; holding brushes, passing paint, even adding her own little touches. Soon Rachel had taken to setting up a second easel nearby for Sarah to work alongside her.

From the earliest she knew she had the flair. Soon she surpassed her mother in technical ability and artistry. And her ability to paint had been much developed. She had gone to art school and worked alongside famous painters. Not only did she paint beautiful scenery, but much else besides. At times, when the mood took her, she would paint with photographic detail. Other times she wanted to evoke primeval forces and her paintings were combinations of light and dark, blurred shapes and overpowering colours, bordering on grotesque.

People recognised and applauded her talent, awards and paintings hung in major galleries. Still her fondest pleasures were in the quick book-sized pictures she made and sold immediately in the markets, done in the moment and of anything that took her fancy.

But her mother had something too.

Of all the favourite paintings that she owned, and there were many, it was one her Mum had done, painted one spring when Sarah, herself, was a teenager, that remained most special.

It was like a view from this house, but not quite real. It looked down on people having a picnic in the park below, distant boats on the harbour and, at the edge of the park was a boat tied to the jetty, facing out to sea, a blue hull and tiny red writing on the stern – too small to actually read, but looking like three words joined together. People at the picnic were celebrating, you could tell from the way they stood, the way they moved and looked at each other and out across the view. You knew it was a special happy occasion.

Towards the centre were two women talking together, clearly mother and daughter, the small to medium sized bodies, neat full figures wearing brightly coloured dresses, seen from the side. The one woman with a cloud of brown golden hair, with red highlights where the sun caught it; the other with hair much the same, but washed with grey. She knew, watching as her mother painted, and without being told, that they were her grandmother, Maria, and her great grandmother, Alison.

But it was not so much the colour and the light that set the picture apart. It was the vital life force that flowed between these two central figures. She knew that, with all her ability and success, here was something well beyond anything she had ever painted, it was better than her best.

At last, a year after her mother gave her the story, she knew what she would do. Perhaps it would be as good. She would paint them as she could now see them in her mind, that same day but now each half turned to face forwards, facing towards each other, but gazing out to a place of shared memories over a distant horizon. In the centre of their memories sat a long lost girl, dark haired girl, lost in a sky where she was barely a shadow. But she was there, buried within memory was her story, seeking to live again

She set to work and in five days the painting was done. She knew, as she walked away from it, to put away her brushes, that this was, to her at least, her best work. It had transformed their memories into her memory. Now a life force of together shared imagination would live on, an old story retold, brought alive by the words her mother had spoken on that last day.

There was a space next to her mother's picture, high on the timber living room wall. It had been waiting all these years for something to fill it. That was where this picture belonged.

As she moved into her later life many people would come to visit and sit with her, side by side, in a chair next to the fire. As they lifted their gaze these two paintings would capture their eyes. Many asked their story. She would tell about the one her mother painted, but of hers she would shrug and say, "That's just some old thing I found, but before you ask it's not for sale as I rather like it."

Now remembering back to Rachel's story she was glad to know where all her family had come from and what they all knew about this girl, Sophie. She, who would have been her aunt, had she lived. Instead she was caught forever in a glass frame. This figure needed to be given a chance to move to a life in a place beyond a picture, no longer the small girl in the communion dress, held forever young.

Even though she had looked at Sophie's picture a hundred times on the mantel in her Gran's big house, it was like the picture on the front of a book that was closed. If she could pass her story to another then perhaps that image would be enough, but there was no other to tell. She knew that now the book had to be opened and fully read before it could be closed and put away. She must do something yet for this to happen.

She understood what was needed and that was why she was troubled. The story had come to her, like a mixture of sunlight and shadow, much of it told of happiness but a dark space sat at the centre. When she was little she had heard of Sophie, but not really known about her. Her great-aunt Heather had told her the simple story, but at the end the question remained.

Sometimes, before that day, she had asked her Mum for more, but her Mum would not answer, she did not want to say. So that door of pain stayed locked tight, until almost the end. With all her being, she wanted to unlock that door. But how to do it and what would be found?

It was like an unfinished painting; it sat there and troubled her. Brush strokes and colour and people across part of the canvass, but at its centre a place that sat empty, where nothing dwelt but a shadow. She needed to take up her brush again and finish that part of the picture. But first she needed to see, in her own mind, a real image to paint there.

She must find and know for herself the real Sophie, the person who was alive beyond this photo. That way she could create in her mind her own real picture, a thing she could turn into paint on canvas. Doing that would let her remake and bring back to life Sophie as a finished, complete person.

It would be her final picture, one in which Sophie's and her own life both reached places of understanding, closure on behalf of all who had known and grieved for this girl, trapped in glass for over a hundred years.

Chapter 23 - Closing the Circle

I have this riddle teasing at the edges of my mind. It draws me forever on.

We found out about a little missing girl, Sophie. She lived in our house a century ago. We saw her picture; we held the perfume bottle she might have owned. As we touched these things with our hands, Sophie seemed to reach out and touch us back. It was as if a part of her lived on.

In the months that followed I set out to find out more about her. I found out a few things; her full name, the name of the friend she went missing with. It seemed neither of these children was ever found. I needed other clues.

As I was busy I knew I should let it go. Sophie was nothing to do with me, so why bother? She was just a child who lived in our house a long time ago.

But, as the weeks and months pass, her face in the photo still jumps into my mind, often at unexpected times. I try to say to her, "Leave me in peace!"

It seems she does not agree; this resurgent Sophie Williams. Whenever she enters my mind it is as if she is speaking to me, trying to say an important thing. Slowly this mind image turns into a realisation.

She is determined that her story be known, it is incomplete. My role is to gain and pass on knowledge of what happened, where she went. That way a part of her can come back to life and bring her story to its end, let it finish.

So I persist in my search of what happened to this little lost girl, Sophie. Gradually I find more clues; a title search shows the land on which our house stands was first subdivided and sold to Michael Williams in 1872. When he bought this land his occupation was listed as a builder's labourer. Our house was next sold to Robert McNeil in

1927, sold to Gordon Brown 1938 and after that to a succession of others, until it came to us.

I seem to recall the McNeil name. I realise that Mathew McNeil was the name of the ten year old boy who went missing with Sophie, as listed in the newspaper. Perhaps another clue, although it is not obvious what it means and why Mr Williams, if alive in 1927, would sell his house to Mr McNeil. But, at least, I am getting some names to follow.

About a month after I get this clue I locate a birth certificate for Sophie Williams, born on the tenth of June 1900, to a Mr James Williams and Mrs Maria Williams (born Maria Buller). So I have a mother and father to follow. Maria and James are listed as born in Balmain, with ages and occupations; James was a labourer, Maria was a shopkeeper. Both were born after the house was first built so I suspect that James was Michael's son.

Going back further is more difficult, records are harder to find. In due course I am confident I will find James and Maria's birth certificates. For now I want to know much more of the world in which they lived, the many things happening at the time, to place them in their society.

I think a visit to the Balmain Historical Association and the local library may help. At first this yields little, no obvious connections to the Buller name; but of course, when girls get married, they can move to new places and their names often change. The Williams name is way too common; Michael and James are hardly rare variants. It seems as if every second English and Welsh migrant of the period carried the Williams name. But perhaps Mr Williams, builder, might narrow it.

In the local library, as I am flicking through historical photos, I pause over one taken of building the Balmain Town Hall, pictured partly constructed. Several men stand in front, posing. It is dated 1888. A caption on the back lists; Architect, E. H. Buchannan, and names the others in the picture. Two names which jump out are J. Roberts and M. Williams. The way these two stand together it looks like they were friends. Could this be the same Michael Williams who bought the land for the Smith St house? If he was became a builder it is likely he built it. Perhaps he and Mr Roberts worked together.

Now I have two names. Both may well have been people of note if they worked on such a landmark building. I go back to the Historical Association and ask for clues on how I might find out about well known builders in the 1870-1890 era. We turn up records for a house and hotel built by Mr Jim Roberts and Mr Mike Williams in 1882 and 1884 respectively. Judging by the Town Hall picture in 1888 they look like men in their forties. So it is likely they were married by then with children. It makes sense to me that Michael built the Smith St house after he bought the land in 1872 and then lived there, having a son named James who was the father of Sophie.

With more help from the Historical Association I locate the Marriage Registers for Balmain's churches for the period from 1870 to 1875. I start with the Anglican Church and bingo, there it is, another clue, James Roberts marries Margaret Mitchell in April 1873. I look for that month in the local paper and again a strike.

There is a feature article, in the next edition after the wedding date. 'Prominent local builder, Jim Roberts, marries his sweetheart, Margaret Mitchell.' There is even a photo, old and faded but still clear, showing the bridal party. The man is the same and I am unsurprised that his best man is Michael Williams. The bridesmaid is one 'Rosemary Williams'.

I feel I have hit gold. And there is much more. The article, written by a reporter with a romantic bent, describes how Jim had been Michael's best man, and Margie had been Rosie's bridesmaid at their own wedding of a few months previous. This new love had sprung from their bridal duties together at their friends wedding, held at the Catholic Church on November 6th of the previous year. As it is now Jim and Margie's turn the paper wishes them 'all felicitations'.

It continues, 'The happy couple are moving to their house in Smith St, just down the road from that of their friends Rosie and Mick. Rosie is now expecting her first child. It is hoped that soon there will be similar joyous news for Jim and Maggie.' (*Is this a hint about one on the way?* I think)

So I find the Catholic wedding register, Year 1872. There it is. 'Michael Williams marries Rosemary Martin; Mother Sophia Martin (nee Rodriguez: occupation - wife), Father - Edward Martin, (deceased), occupation - former Ship's Captain – Adelie; representative of the father and witness - Jose Rodriguez, uncle to the bride.'

There is something in the names, 'Adelie', and 'Captain Martin' which rings a bell. I have seen them both somewhere before. So I go back through the books I had been searching recently, nothing there.

Then I go to the old newspapers. Here it is; front page story of October, 1871 in the Sydney Morning Herald.

'Feared ship wreck of the Adelie, in the far Southern Ocean, about 1000 miles east of the Cape of Good Hope, has been confirmed by debris collected by the Marguerite, en route to Melbourne from Cape Town. The Adelie has been overdue for almost a month giving great concern at its fate. Adelie's Captain, Edward Martin, is renowned for his punctuality and seamanship.

'The fate of the Adelie is now tragically resolved with the discovery of a small amount of wreckage from the ship, including part of one lifeboat with the name painted on it.

'The crew of Marguerite reported they had seen indications of a huge storm which passed though this region a few days before and, after discovery of the debris, Marguerite further searched the area for a few days, but no sign of any survivors was found.'

The paper concludes, 'It is, sadly, almost certain that Captain Martin and all his crew perished. May God have mercy on their souls!

'This newspaper has been overwhelmed with condolences for the loss of the Captain and his crew, most of whom have families in Sydney. We extend our deepest sympathies to the families of all who sailed on this ship and, in particular, to Captain Martin's beloved wife Sophia and his daughter Rosie who live in that well known residence in Montague Street, near the corner of Darling St, Balmain.

'May God comfort them all in their sorrows!

'A special service of commemoration will be held at St Augustine's Catholic Church, Balmain, on the 30th September 1871.'

So I think I have found more of the family of James, father of Sophie.

Now I set out to trace Maria's family. The name of Buller is not one I have found in Balmain, but I discover it was known at Millers Point, being the name given to a shipyard that operated from 1847 until the 1930s.

According to an early maritime history book this company, begun at Mace's Wharf in Sussex Street in 1830, was first named, 'McVey Brothers, Shipwrights'. In 1847 it moved to premises in Gas Lane, off Kent Street. At this time it changed its name to 'Rodgers and Buller', due to the ill health of its founder, well known shipping identity, Tom McVey. He had founded the company with his brother Rodger in 1830. Tom became sole proprietor on the death of his brother five years later. In 1854 the company changed its name again, to 'Buller's Shipyard and Engineering Works'. And there is more, a statement that Mr McVey and Mr Rodgers lived in Balmain, just across the water and easily accessible to their yard by small boat.

This history book also records that, in 1854, Mr Rodgers moved to Newcastle to establish a new iron foundry and shipping engineers firm and, after this, Mr Buller carried on the business alone. Subsequently Mr Buller was joined in his business by his sons, Charles and Robert, who carried on the business after the Mr Buller senior's death.

The article continues, 'Unfortunately the tragic death, in 1907, of Mr Charles Buller and his wife Alison, nee Rodgers, residents of East Balmain, saw the beginning of the slow decline of the business. Charles Buller was a great innovator and had modernised the business, seeing it reach its peak success in the early 1900s when it had a workforce of more than 100 men, and extensive machinery including state of the art steam machinery and early electric cranes and tools. Mr Robert Buller continued the business until his death in 1930 but, in later years, the business declined from its major role in Sydney's maritime industry, as it failed to continue the modernisation which Charles had commenced.

Further information follows about the Rodgers shipping works and foundry in Newcastle, including the death of Mr Archibald Rodgers from tetanus, in 1870 and the subsequent death of his son James in 1924, who continued the business after his father's death.

So now I have a Balmain connection to the Buller name in Charles Buller, with him listed as an East Balmain resident when he died.

Alison Rodgers also seems significant, with both a Balmain connection and perhaps a relationship by descent to the Mr Rodgers who was in early partnership with Mr Buller and lived in Balmain before moving to Newcastle. I am certain I have seen another reference to Alison Rodgers somewhere.

Again an old book turns it up. This time it is 'Early Sandstone Houses of the Balmain Peninsula'. It shows old photos of significant sandstone buildings in the period 1840 to 1900, and lists their owners, as of 1900. I examine the title page and it turns out the book was republished by the Balmain Historical Association in the 1980s, when it sought to bring outdated information on ownership up to date.

Returning to this book I find it, half way through, a picture of a grand sandstone house, Ocean View, in East Balmain. Over the page is a second photo from the back of the house, of a garden which plunges down to a stunning view out across the harbour. The owner is listed, in 1900, as Alison Rodgers. So I have a two way connection between the Rodgers and Buller names. Unsurprisingly the house was originally that of Tom and Mary McVey. Their will passed it to Alison Rodgers on their death. This makes me almost certain that this Alison was from the Rodgers family who were in the original shipping business in Sussex Street and Gas Lane. Perhaps, after her father's death, she returned to Sydney and married her family friend or childhood sweetheart, Charles, who was a child of the original Mr Buller.

Soon I am on the track of more information about the fate of Alison Rodgers and Charles Buller, their death by shipwreck on the rocks near Greymouth, New Zealand is reported in the Sydney Morning Herald in September 1907, getting close to the time that Sophie disappeared. The same story gives the final link. 'Mrs and Mrs Buller (nee Rodgers) are survived by their three children, son John and daughters Heather and Maria, and by their many grandchildren."

I feel a picture is beginning to emerge, if not of Sophie then at least of where she came from. The Rodgers connection intrigues me. I cannot really remember, but something is tucked in my distant memory of my own family having a connection to the Rodgers name in Newcastle.

I also discover that Alison Rodgers owned a small timber cottage, Roisin, in East Balmain, near where Paul Street joins Weston St. I think I know this cottage, having seen it when walking around East Balmain, or at least I have seen a place which matches its description, a place with a garden full of sprawling pink and yellow roses, as befits its old Scottish name, Roisin.

With the death of Alison Rodgers the house, 'Ocean View', passed to her daughter Maria Williams in 1910, and to Maria's daughter, Rachel McMillan, on Maria's death in 1956. On Rachel's death, in 1983, the house passed to her daughter, Sarah, who at the time lived in the same timber cottage, Roisin, in East Balmain. Here the family connection to 'Ocean View' ends. Sarah sold this sandstone house a few months later, continuing to reside in Roisin.

That was 25 years ago. Does Sarah McMillan still live in her little timber cottage? If so she must be around 80. And, if she is still there, does she know anything about what happened to Sophie? By my calculation Sophie was her aunt. Perhaps a family story still exists to tell what happened.

But now I am struck by uncertainty. Is it fair to ask Sarah McMillan what happened to her mother's sister, Sophie, all those long years ago? If still, after all this time, no one knows what happened, will it only reopen old wounds, rekindle painful memories of people who want to forget?

I consider walking to Sarah's house and knocking on the door to try and find out. But something restrains me. I do not feel entitled to put my nose into private grief and human tragedy, merely out of prurient interest.

So I let it sit, temporarily putting my investigation into a hiatus. There are other leads I could follow, but I have a moral doubt which infects my pursuit. And there I leave it untouched for almost a year.

One day I find myself in Newcastle, visiting my dear old Aunt Edith, sister of my dead mother, Helen, and keeper of our family's memories.

Something brings Sophie's story and the Rodgers connection to it into my mind. I say to Edith, "Some years ago you told me something about the name Rodgers. I think you said there was a family connection in Newcastle, but I can't remember what it was. Can you remind me?"

I see Edith looking at me in a surprisingly deep and meaningful way. She does not answer. After a second she goes to her spare bedroom. I hear the sound of rustling papers.

In a minute she comes out with two single sheets of paper, slightly dog eared documents. She passes across the first one in silence.

I read it; a date of 1870 and the header of the Newcastle Chronicle. It describes the death of Mr Archibald Rodgers, his hand crushed in his iron foundry, it becoming gangrenous, then amputated, but a day later tetanus had set in. I know this story, or at least a part of it. It is the story of Alison Rodgers father.

Edith passes me the second sheet, names arranged in a family tree. It begins with Archibald and Hannah Rodgers and their children, James, John, Archibald, Alison, Hannah, (junior) and Alexander. It shows Hannah deceased in 1849. Archibald remarries Helen McLaren in 1850; their children: Helen, Agnes and Anne. The penny drops. I do not have to read further.

This is not the story of some unknown man called Archibald Rodgers; this is the story of my great-great grandfather. The instant I see the second wife, Helen McLaren, and her daughter, Helen, I know. My mum was Helen, and her grandmother was Helen. She was that Helen, the daughter of Archibald Rodgers and Helen McLaren.

Now the family story comes flooding back. Archibald's daughter, Helen, left Newcastle after her father's death from tetanus. She became a school teacher in Bathurst. Her son was my grandfather. This is my story. Alison was my great grandmother's half sister. Sophie, her granddaughter, shares my genes; she is blood, a relative to me and to Tara.

Could Sophie have somehow called to Tara, directing her to find her precious things, even after all these years. It does not feel like co-incidence, but rather like invisible threads pulling us both to strange yet familiar places through warps in time and space. Goosebumps and chills run along my arms and down my spine. I just have to know!

I look up; my aunt is still standing there, looking at me with her quizzical look. I have not spoken since she found the papers.

I say, "Archibald Rodgers was my great-great grandfather, was he not?"

She nods. "But of course, I thought you knew."

So I sit her down and tell her the story or, at least, the parts I know.

Edith gives a faint frown, trying to remember, then her face clears, "I remember now. It was a family story when I was a little girl. The family knew that Sophie had gone missing and was never found, but no one ever knew why or how.

"When I was a little girl I stayed at Ocean View in Balmain for a few days once. My Aunty Maria and Uncle Jimmy, that is what I called them, as we were all connected by Archibald, still lived there then.

"I had come from the country to school in Sydney with Helen (my Mum). At first we had stayed with my Aunty Ada, but then she died of a stroke. So Maria and Jimmy came over to get us. They brought me and Helen to their house in Balmain, and we stayed there for a few days until we could go back home to Warialda.

"Maria and Jimmy were lovely warm people. They treated me like a grandchild. On the mantel in Ocean View was a picture of Sophie. When I asked about the picture Maria sat me down on a chair and told me what they knew. It was not much more than what you have said; that Sophie had gone missing with her friend Mathew and they had never found her.

"As she spoke I saw Jimmy had tears in his eyes. After a minute Maria went over and put her hand on his shoulder and she had tears in her eyes too. They said that, even after all those years and having all their other children, they still missed her, but were not really sad anymore, because she was happy in another place.

"Although they said she was happy now, I could tell that not knowing what had really happened to Sophie had left a huge hole inside them, more than thirty years later the pain was still so raw."

Edith pauses for a minute, lost in this memory, before going on, "Their daughter, Rachel, lived in a cottage nearby. Sometimes we went there and played with her daughter, Sarah, who was my half cousin. Sarah was about Helen's age; other times Sarah and Rachel came to Ocean View.

"I have not heard of Sarah for years, but someone would have told me if she died. I think Sarah also has a brother, Tom, who lives in New York."

"I will get you the rest of my papers about the Rodgers family, there is quite a bit as they were famous Newcastle people. One of my cousins has been researching their lives. She has given me a copy of what she found out."

Edith goes again to her room and comes back with a stack of papers, an inch thick, for me to read.

Then she says "Could I come back to Sydney with you? I would like to see the perfume bottle, I have not heard about it before, and it would be nice to see a picture of Sophie again and visit my old playmate, Sarah."

So that is it. I bring Edith to our house and she stays in Tara's room. I wonder if Sophie's presence will speak to her too.

That night I sit and read these papers. I start to truly understand who my great-great grandparents were and their links to Sophie's story; she the half great-great aunt I never knew, now the forever child, age of my daughter. She calls to me now from beyond the grave as a vanished eight year old girl. Her voice says to tell her story.

Chapter 24 – Bringing the children home

Next day we go round to visit Sarah. I ask Edith if we should try to find her number and ring first.

"Oh, don't worry about that rubbish," she says. "She is my cousin, after all. Seeing she is old like me, she is not likely to be gone out or too busy."

So we go there.

The door opens. Before me stands an old lady, genteel and gracious, but with a touch of wildness. Those eyes, Sophie's eyes, stare out at me, only a hundred years on. I do not know how I know that the eyes in a tiny black and white photo are the same. But in my heart and soul I know this lady carries Sophie's likeness in this part, even yet.

Sarah knows Edith at once, even after all these years. She invites us in. Edith simply introduces me as the son of her sister, Helen, who Sarah played with those many years ago.

But I swear Sarah looks at me with an insight that says she knows I am more than that. She indicates for me to bring an extra chair. She and Edith take two much loved chairs by the fire, while I sit between them.

As I raise my eyes from their faces, to the place above the fire, it is like the whole story comes alive in vivid colour. There are two paintings, one of a picnic with boats behind. In the centre are two ladies talking, as if awaiting their departure. The other painting shows the same two ladies, closer up, but with a similar background, half talking and half gazing out to sea. They look to a familiar, long remembered horizon and somehow this horizons tells of another person, little more than suggestion and shadow, but yet there is clearly a presence there that sits both outside and within their memories. I realise, unsaid, that this shadow is a long lost person, a child unknown. I am captivated by my past family.

I do not have to ask, who are these people, the people of the picture story? They look as vibrant and alive as if I was standing there talking to them. I know, unspoken, they are Alison, grandmother, and Maria, mother of Sophie. I know it with certainty, even though I have never seen either. And somehow I also know that the partial shadow is a memory of Sophie.

I realise, after a minute of staring, transfixed, that Sarah is talking to me. As I look back to her, there it is again, that same smile and those same eyes. Creatures of her and my flesh are alive, above her on canvass.

So, before we talk, the unspoken bond is made; to seek and discover the truth which I will try to tell in words and she will tell in a final picture.

Then Sarah and I talk together while Edith listens. I tell her the little I have found out, and of our new house. Sarah tells us the story she got through her Mum, most of which is written in this book.

The final thing she says is. "One thing that has really stuck in my mind, since my Mum, Rachel, told me this story many years ago. It is what she said just after she finished telling the rest."

"She said, 'I really wished that Gran Alison had lived until after Sophie had gone, because I knew, deep down inside, that she would know where Sophie went. It was like they were kindred souls, different outside but forged in the same crucible of love and fire.'

"I don't know how it helps, but it seemed she was saying I had to find out about my great-grandmother and that may give a missing clue. I have looked through all the things of hers that were passed down through our family but I am no wiser. Perhaps you can see something that escapes my tired old eyes."

I try to think too but nothing comes to me. I shake my head.

Sarah says, "It is not a question for today, but do keep looking, still.

Then she asks to see the perfume bottle. I give it to her and she holds it, warm in her hand, for a long, long time. Her face grows still and calm, as something flows between her and that tiny little bottle. It is like she is taken to another place, her face glowing with a strange happy light, while tears trickle slowly down her cheeks.

She takes off the bottle top, inhales the smell, saying "Oh it brings it all back, those happy, golden days of my childhood. I am glad it has been passed along the chain to your family. Perhaps one day your daughter too will have need of this."

I say to her. "These are yours, you are her nearest kin."

She looks at me and says. "Perhaps they are mine but, if I was meant to have them, then I think Maria would have given them to me herself. I am not sure, but for now I would like you to keep them in your care."

We say our goodbyes knowing we must both keep looking until we find the missing piece. I have gained so much understanding but still no closure. Where did Sophie and her friend Matty go, all those many years ago?

So I return to the Historical Association. There is a lady sitting at the table who I do not know. As I rummage, seeking inspiration, she looks up at me. So I tell her some parts of the story. When I mention an Alison who lived in Balmain long ago, she says.

"There is something, though I am not sure if it will help you. About ten years ago, it was on New Year's Eve, when the crowd was gathering at East Balmain; a couple set up their picnic at the edge of the rocks in the park to the east of the ferry wharf. It was somewhere about here," she says, pointing to a map showing the end of Paul Street where the park starts.

She continues. "They decided to go for a walk, while they were waiting for the fireworks, but they wanted to leave their valuable things somewhere safe, to save carrying them. They saw a small space in the rocks, behind where they were sitting. In the entrance of the space one of the rocks was loose, just sitting there in the start of the hole. So they pulled it out, to put their things behind it.

Behind the rock they found a small tin box. Inside was what appeared to be a little girl's diary. It was wrapped in oilcloth. It had the name 'Alison' written on it. They thought it might be important so they brought it here. From the type of paper we know it dates to around 1850. I looked at some of it and it seemed to me to be a small girl's meanderings and dreaming, from when she was about five or six years old. It talks about a few things, like a secret cave, a small black friend Ruthie and a magic perfume bottle of memories."

I feel a surge of wild irrational excitement. "Could I see it please,? I say.

She goes and finds it, then gives it to me. It is a metal box as described, dark and tarnished but solid. Inside is an object about six inches by four inches and an inch thick, wrapped in its oilcloth cover. I unwrap a book. The faded pink cover has a small girl's hand writing. It says the name 'Alison'.

Almost reverentially I open the cover. I gaze at the writing, now over 160 years old, of my great grandmother's half sister. The first page starts.

"I am so happy. It is my birtday and I am 5. My Mummy has given me this for a preset to write in."

A few pictures are on the next two pages; then I turn to the next page after with a jolt.

"Today we buried my Mummy. She died last night. I trying not to cry, but I miss her so bad."

To the next page, "Today I am even more unhappy. My brother Archie who is 9 has died too. He was my best friend and I miss him so much. He was very sad too when Mummy died but we tried to help each other be brave. And now he is buried next to Mummy. But the worse thing is how it is hurting Daddy, like two holes in his heart."

Then the next entry, "My Daddy went away on the boate today. I am trying not to cry while I write, I don't know if I will ever see him again. But he gave me a special present, a blue-green bottle, like the sea with waves on it. It was Mummies. When I open it I can smell her and I am happy, but I still want to cry. So when I was crying I put my tears in the bottle and I think it will help me be strong."

Then an entry with a description about what her Gran Mary had told her about the bottle. Followed by "Now I understand how I can put my happy memories in it. I will fill it up so full so when Daddy comes home I can make him happy."

Then a bit further on, "Daddy came home today. Hooray I am so excited, I want to dance and shout."

Then the next entry, "Today I met Mrs Helen, she is sad too because her hubsand died. But I made a special promise with her. We will both try not to be sad."

Then, "I know Mrs Helen likes Daddy and I think Daddy likes her too. That is good because Mummy is not here anymore and she would want little Hannah and Alexander to have a new mummy."

About half the diary was filled with her little notes and memories getting longer as the years passed, about her school friends and other people, and what she did and liked.

Then a little black girl called Ruthie starts to appear. She describes how Ruthie and her would go exploring and 'search the shores for tressures.'

Then something electric, 'Ruthie and I found a little cave. Only we know and we have both promised we will not tell anyone else about it.'

From the description I am almost sure they are describing Ballast Point. I don't know why I am so sure, but I know, with no doubt, this is the clue Sarah and I have been looking for.

Perhaps it is another chance discovery like many along the path I have followed for the past many months. Perhaps Alison has reached out her hands alongside Sophie out to bring us to this place. Yet it is so.

Now, with total certainty, I set out on the last part of my journey.

I search the archives for the history of Ballast Point, and discover work was done on the installation of a tank there at about the time the children disappear. I finally find a work assignment for two workers Fred Jones and Joe Wilson, who are each paid five pounds by a shipping company to level the site and prepare it for a tank and jetty to be built. A week after the work begins I find in the site's log book the notation. "Today Mr Frederick Jones took two charges of dynamite to shift a large rock which is preventing the levelling being completed". It is dated September 3rd, 1908.

This is the last day the children are seen. My mind sees a picture of two little children in a cave below. I feel unutterably sad.

I continue my research. There are now the remains of three big tanks there and they don't sound original. There is no longer a scrubby edge to the headland, it has all been removed.

Finally I track down documents relating to the installation of the new tanks, in 1942, from Navy Archives. I am like a dog with a bone. I can't leave it, there must be more. Buried amongst Navy reports of the construction, is a hand written notation, 'Works delayed for two hours today. Military Police called. Remains found under rocks removed and report lodged to police'

Police archives defeat me. Then I think. *Perhaps the remains were lodged with the coroner. I think their archives should be in a retrievable form.*

I manage to locate Glebe coroner's records, which appear to be the most likely place of dispatch at that time. I open a heavy bound book that records the incomings and outgoings in 1942. There it is, two days after the Military Police site visit.

'Remains of two children and associated goods found at Ballast Point, Balmain. Lodged with report A109201-42, stored in Bay 23, container 5.'

Yet more investigation; this storage area no longer exists but a custody chain does. My search leads to an old warehouse in western Sydney. The accession clerk confirms the location and currency of the record.

'Transferred in 1963, last review of evidence 1942.'

I realise I am at the end of the trail. I am not sure if I want to know what this container holds. I think, *What help will it bring? Who will benefit after all this time?* But I need to know and Edith and Sarah deserve to know too. As the nearest living relatives to this time and place, at least they can represent those who suffered the loss and accept its closure.

I ring them to inform them of what I have found. They say, "Go on."

We walk along air conditioned corridors, the attendant and I. There is a faint anaesthetic hum. We come to the marked bay and then to the marked cubicle and then to a shelf and drawer.

It is opened and I know with total certainty this is them.

The piles of broken bones lie mingled in death as in the final moments of life. It is the blue bird that convinces me, told from Maria, to Rachel, to Sarah, a tale of Matty's loving gift to Sophie, the pledge of their friendship.

An exquisite fairy wren, colours and detail perfect, carved and received with such love. I feel its soul soar and fly free with the spirits of these two children, going to a place of peace and happiness. This is the secret of the perfume bottle, that when all else passes such love remains.

A month later we gather all the family members we can find; Rodgers, Smiths, Wilsons, Campbells, McNeils, McVeys, Bullers, Williams and Martins, and others too, including aboriginal custodians of the land one of whom is a man who is an almost direct descendant of little Ruthie, great grandchild of her cousin. Sadly Ruthie died young with no children of her own. But this man is a descendant of her grandfather, Jimmy, and is the living custodian of the echidna totem. So he will take the precious engraved wooden bowl that has passed through hands both black and white, since its making, and return it to its true owners.

On this day we form a sombre gathering at the place where the last remains of these two small children were found, standing in a semi-cirlce on this rock headland and gazing out from a hillside vista so different to what these children last saw, no bushes or cave remain now.

We have approval of the Council and the other officials to place a small casket with the two children's remains, cemented into the rock of Ballast Point, covered with a plaque bearing their names.

Fittingly the Point is now a place for people to enjoy, fashioned into the shape of a ship, which waits, as if to carry them to another far off land.

Sarah, body frail in the spring breeze, stands at end of the point, above the small casket and holds the small blue bird aloft to the bright blue sky.

Her voice carries to us all, tired and thin, but resonant. "This bird is the symbol of our family having finally reached a place of understanding and peace. I ask it to fly free and bring these two dear spirits across space and time into a joyous eternity."

I thought then perhaps she would fling the small blue bird into the sky so it too could fly away. Instead she walks quietly to me. She stands and stares at me with those sad, but smiling, eyes which search my soul. She speaks in a soft voice that only I can hear. It may be my imaginings but it is as if small Sophie is talking to me.

The voice says. "Please take this small blue bird and, with my perfume bottle and picture, place them in the place from whence they came, as put there by Maria. Perhaps, in some time and place beyond all our knowledge, another small person will have need of them.

"And would you write this story as you have discovered it, to travel along with them too."

I know, without any words spoken, that Sarah will paint her last picture. Spaced around its frame are three remembered old Balmain houses holding their families' stories. The space in the centre holds four much loved children; Sophie, Mathew, little Alison and a small black friend, all met again, finding treasures on sea shores; dreams carried aloft on the tiny wings of a small blue bird.

When our ceremony is finished we take the blue bird, the perfume bottle and the small sepia photo and place them all on the ledge of the chimney in the old Balmain house.

Now I have written it, just these words, it is complete.

I know Sarah has painted her picture though I need not see it. My mind already holds its clear image.

I place my words into a tightly sealed package. It rests alongside these other things, in the chimney of the house, perhaps one day to be read again, perhaps to pass into dust. I think these words are like the feathers of the brightly painted blue bird. Together they can fly free and carry our many linked souls through time and space and into eternity.

Epilogue

It is now six months since I have finished writing. I thought I had fully told Sophie's story.

But today I discover how stories have a strange ability to keep going on, passing through yet more generations and crossing into other families' lives, other people who have also shared in the history of this house.

I am working at my desk when I hear a knocking sound. I open the front door. Standing outside are four ladies, three in a line and one behind. I know at once, by their looks and an imperceptible kindred thing, that they are all related and connected to this house. The oldest woman is perhaps in her eighties, with the sprightly good-mannered bearing of generations past. The next lady looks in her sixties. She has the most striking and captivating face, not quite beautiful, but such presence, magnetic eyes which draw you in. The third lady, mature but still young, carries an aura of hard earned wisdom with her. Behind her is the youngest woman, I think it is her daughter. She has a waif like face, framed by spiky hair, and a twenty something body.

I say, "Hello, How can I help you?"

The middle lady speaks on behalf of the others, saying, "You don't know us but we lived in this house before you, my mother and I when I was a child in the 1950s and 60s. It was also my daughter', Catherine's, home for a while. My mother continued to live here until she sold the house in the late 1980s. I used the front room where Sophie lived and she was my childhood friend. Sophie was my daughter's friend too, even though we then lived on the opposite side of Australia. Later Sophie became my daughter and granddaughter Amelie's friend when they needed help.

"We came to the ceremony for Sophie and Matty, on that day at Ballast Point, but we did not want to intrude; it was a day for their own families.

But it made us remember our time living here and how important Sophie was in our lives. For the last six months we have written our story, in which Sophie has a central role. Today we wondered if you would tell to us the rest of the story that you found out about her life.

With that I invite them in for tea and tell them this story. In return they pass me the hand written manuscript of their story. When they depart I sit down and read it, barely leaving my seat over a day and night.

As I finish and lay it aside I feel I have found a fitting closure to Sophie' story, the girl in the picture with only eight years of living, but a child whose presence has passed across many generations and may yet continue.

With my reading done I place their manuscript alongside the words I have written, to share the same journey into Sophie's future.

Those who want to know more the books Lizzie's Tale and Devil's Choice, continue this story.

Appendix 1 : The Truth Behind the Imaginings

The perfume bottle described in this book is a product of my imagination. However this story is based on truth in some places as follows:

The arrival of my great-great grandfather in Sydney in 1841 is true, with what I know, as compiled by other relatives, as follows.

"Archibald Alexander Rodgers was born on 4th April 1814, at Barnyards village in Scotland. He was the fifth of seven children of James Rodger and Eupan Bruce. In 1841, Archibald Rodger travelled to Sydney, with his wife Hannah and their two children James and Archibald, arriving on the "William Turner" on October 5th. Archibald Junior's twin brother John died in the United Kingdom before they left. In Australia they had further children Alison, Hannah and Alexander. Archibald was listed on arrival as "Blacksmith, Presbyterian, aged 27, can read and write". Hannah was listed at the same time as "Dressmaker, Presbyterian, 24 years, can read and write"

In Sydney Archibald worked in an engineering business, 'Roger McVey and Company, Shipsmith', at Mace's Wharf in Sussex St, Sydney. In 1847 the partnership became 'Rodgers and Buller, Engineers', in Gas St, then later 'A Rodger, Engineer and Shipsmith', Gas Lane, off Kent St North.

Hannah died at Balmain, in Sydney, in March 1849 and Archibald Junior died soon after, in June 1849. Shortly after their deaths Archibald sailed back to England on the 'Sarah', returning on the same ship to Sydney on 10th December 1849. With him came his younger brother William, William's wife, Isabella, and their son. Also on board the ship were Colin McLaren and his wife, Helen. Colin died of cholera on the voyage.

Three months later Archibald Rodgers and Helen McLaren were married in Sydney. Their first child, Margaret, only lived for two weeks. Their next child, also named Helen, was my grandfather's mother.

In 1854 they moved to Newcastle and Archibald founded an engineering works, 'Iron and Brass Foundry and General Iron Works', at Honeysuckle Point, in lower Church St. This is now King St and the site of Newcastle City Hall and Civic Centre. In Newcastle they had three daughters, listed as born at the Foundry; Helen, Agnes and Anne. Archibald died of tetanus in 1870, after his hand was crushed in an accident at the Foundry, as told in the Newcastle Herald extract in Chapter 9."

I know nothing further of his life in Balmain. Of the real Hannah I have discovered a photo of a pretty lady with dark hair, not the lady of the fair hair and complexion I imagined, though in other respects the similarity to my imagination is strong. This picture conveys to me a self-possessed woman, who, in a mere 32 years of life, had 6 children, crossed the world and established a new life for herself and her family. Her own mother is also named Alison, so my idea of Hannah's first daughter being named for her mother is right.

Of this daughter, Alison, when writing this novel, I knew nothing of her life, except that she was the oldest daughter. Since then I have discovered that she died in Newcastle on the 24th of April 1871, only a few months after her father's death.

So it is like sliding doors, a real Alison, the great aunt I never knew who experienced the real grief and pain of losing her mother, brother, sister and father in her short life, and who never returned from Newcastle. Then there is my imaginary Alison – the mind shadow of what may have been if she lived on. I hope the soul of the real Alison is pleased with my mind's creation. From this unknown child's pain comes the essence of the kind, wise, fun-loving soul who is a central character of my book.

As with Alison, so too with Maria; a person of my imagination; living only in my book. Yet I can see her so clearly, waiting and hoping for her beloved Jimmy to return to her at the old Balmain house. For me she is also the Maria of Joe Dolan's song.

'Who's going to tell Maria he won't return,
Who's going to tell Maria that love can burn'

But she waits still, her hope undimmed; and, as the story teller, I can give her the gift of joy regained.

Our move to Balmain and the purchase of a timber cottage in the locality of Smith Street is true in general if not in all specifics. The basic layout of the house and the pleasure it gave us is as described, as is the wonderful sense of welcome and community we discovered on coming to Balmain.

The discovery of a mass card of a little girl who had lived and died around the same time as Sophie, and which had been hidden in the chimney of our house in Balmain is true, though we did not discover it. I do not know what happened to her, though I have since found out her name was Jessie Holmes. A copy of the photo and the minimal information we know of her is in Appendix 2.

The general locality of Balmain in relation to Sydney City and the streets referred to in Sydney and Balmain are real streets. The Exchange and West End Hotels and the Town Hall are real buildings. I do not know the names of the builders of the Town Hall, though it's year of construction and the name of the architect are correct. The names and locations of churches and schools cited in Balmain are generally correct.

The first people of this part of Sydney at the time of colonisation were the Gadigal clan of the Eora Nation. They were massively decimated by early diseases, particularly small pox but also other diseases brought by the Europeans. The most famous of these were Bennelong and Barangaroo, who lived on an island in the harbour they called Memel, which has been renamed Goat Island. It sits in close proximity to East Balmain and Ballast Point where parts of this story are set. The Gadigal people lived extensively on the seafood bounty of the harbour using bark canoes called nawi and twine and fish hooks called bara. It is likely they ate local fish such as the wulamay or snapper. Other words that have survived include, gunyah for shelter, ganing for cave and duwal for a short two barbed spear suited to catch fish. I use some of these words in the part of my book that tells of Ruthie and her grandfather, Jimmy.

The character, Ruthie, of the Gadigal, is a person of my imagination, with no real basis, nor has the totem she ascribes to her father of the echidna. However this animal was an important animal in broader aboriginal totems and stories as well as a favoured food item, and is depicted in rock engravings within the Sydney region so it is likely to have been a significant animal for Eora clans While the Gadigal clan was massively depleted due to diseases and taking of lands some remnants of the clan are believed to have survived and combined with other clans, living at the margins of European society around Sydney over the mid-1800s until they gradually moved to locations such as La Perouse and Redfern. Hence a remnant of Gadigal peoples living in Blackwattle Bay around the Glebe foreshore, where there would have been an abundance of shellfish is the shallow seas and swamps with freshwater is a reasonable supposition, as is the idea of interactions and bartering with the European community. In addition non aboriginal names were often given to such people by the white people with whom they interacted, as these names were easier for them to say and remember than the aboriginal names.

Ballast Point and Balmain East are real localities on the Balmain Peninsula, though their development bears little resemblance in time or type to that described in the book. Specifically Ballast Point was already substantially cleared and changed before the time cited in this book and fuel tanks were not built until the 1930s. The Navy had no role in their use.

I have no knowledge of a cemetery in East Balmain, though a later cemetery was built in Leichhardt. However it is likely that there was an early cemetery somewhere in locality of East Balmain where Hannah and Archibald Junior were buried in 1849. One day I will try to find out about them, and where they lived and died.

Balmain became a strongly working class area in the early 1900s with a very large number of dock workers living there.

Bubonic plague did occur in Sydney in 1900 with many deaths. I do not know if any plague deaths occurred in Balmain. Similarly, other epidemics of disease occurred in the early history of Sydney.

The Australian Federation Ceremony occurred in 1901, including a march from Hyde Park, which went along Park St, with a crowd of approximately 500,000 onlookers. Sir Henry Parkes lived in Balmain for several years at Hampton Villa and was a leading figure in the movement for the Australian Federation, although he died before it occurred. Edmund Barton was extensively involved in drafting the constitution for the Australian Federation.

A Balmain football team played at Birchgrove Oval in the late 1800s and early 1900s and became an inaugural team in the Rugby League competition established in 1908. It still wears the black and gold tiger colour and retains the Tigers Name, though now as part of the Wests Tigers. I am proud to say I am one of its many later day supporters and still go to watch it play, though now at Leichardt rather than Birchgrove Oval.

Balmain was and remains a village outside of time, centred around its people and the sense of community they create. It is also a repository of many hidden treasures, the beautiful old timber and sandstone houses, undiscovered cobbled lanes twisting between houses and plunging down to the sea, jacarandas in purple flower in spring, glimpsed vistas of hills and harbour, and the boats which quietly float across these views. At night, seen across the water all of Sydney city comes sparkling to life, light filled high rise towers and the dark towering masses of Anzac and Sydney Harbour Bridges.

Along with many thousands of others we watch fireworks on Sydney Harbour Bridge, as viewed from East Balmain and seen on televisions around the world, each New Year's Eve.

The blue bird of my story is the beautiful fairy wren, once common and now seen just occasionally, on the headlands and in the forest fringes at the edges of Balmain. Now people are planting new bushland places for it to live. Perhaps again one day it will be often seen by Balmain's children.

*Dedicated to many people who have lived in
and loved the place we call Balmain,
over countless millennia*

Appendix 2 : Jessie Grace Holmes – Unknown Girl

When I wrote this book, the 'girl in the photo frame' was but a recollection of a photo I had been shown when we bought the house. It was passed on to us by the previous owners who found it in the chimney. We had then put it away for safe keeping and in telling this story I had only a vague memory of its details – being a dark haired eight year old girl who died around 100 years ago. As my memory was unclear and I did not know where we had put the actual photo I used my imagination to create this imaginary person who I named Sophie.

We have now found that real photo. It is a thing much damaged, most likely scorched from many years of chimney heat. However some details still remain visible. I have transcribed these below along with a copy of this photo, broken, with parts missing and other parts illegible.

So now I have her real name, Jessie Grace Holmes, and her age, date of death and the fact she was both a daughter and a sister. Perhaps this Jessie deserves to be brought to life in her own story, something based on whatever real information I can uncover 100 years on. It is a task for another day, but I hope in time to be able to tell the story of the real Jessie Grace Holmes, perhaps to even discover some descendants of this girl and her family who once lived in this Old Balmain House, with their own memories.

THOUGH LOST TO SIGHT FOREVER DEAR

IN LOVING MEMORY OF

Our Dearest Daughter and Our Dearest Sister
Jessie Grace Holmes

Who departed this life Mar1 1916

Dearest Jessie, thou hast left us
Thou dost dwell with angels now
And a wreath of glory priceless
Sparkles on thy shining brow
In thy pure and joyous childhood
Christ called, "Child come here to Me"
Wait a little, dearest Jessie
And we soon shall follow thee

Abide with Me
Memorial Card Company 112 King St Sydney Copyright

About the Author

Graham Wilson lives in Sydney Australia. He has completed and published nine separate books, and also a range of combined novel box sets.

They comprise two series,

1. The Old Balmain House Series – three novels

2 The Crocodile Spirit Dreaming Series – five novels

along with a family memoir, *Children of Arnhem's Kaleidoscope*

The *Old Balmain House Series* starts with this novel, *Little Lost Girl*, which was previously titled, *The Old Balmain House*. Its setting is an old weatherboard cottage, in Sydney, where the author lived for seven years. Here a photo was discovered of a small girl who lived and died about 100 years ago. The book imagines the story of her life and family, based in the real Balmain, an early inner Sydney suburb, with its locations and historical events providing part of the story background. The second novel in this series, *Lizzie's Tale*, builds on the Balmain house setting, It is the story of a working class teenage girl who lives in this same house in the 1950s and 1960s, It tells of how, when pregnant, she is determined not to surrender her baby for adoption and of her struggle to survive in this unforgiving society. The third novel in this series, *Devil's Choice*, follows the next generation of the family in *Lizzie's Tale*. Lizzie's daughter is faced with the awful choice of whether to seek the help of one of her mother's rapists' in trying to save the life of her own daughter who is inflicted with an incurable disease.

The Crocodile Spirit Dreaming Series is based in Outback Australia. The first novel *Just Visiting* tells the story of an English backpacker, Susan, who visits the Northern Territory and becomes captivated and in great danger from a man who loves crocodiles. The second book in the series, *Creature of an Ancient Dreaming*, (previously *The Diary*), follows the consequences of the first book based around the discovery of this man's remains and his diary and Susan, being placed on trial for murder. The third book, *The Empty Place*, is about Susan's struggle to retain her sanity in jail while her family and friends desperately try to find out what really happened on that fateful day before it is too late. In *Lost Girls* Susan vanishes and it tells the story of the search for her and four other lost girls whose passports were found in the possession of the man she killed. The final book in the series, *Sunlit Shadow Dance* is the story of a girl who appears in a remote aboriginal community in North Queensland, without any memory except for a name. It tells how she rebuilds her life from an empty shell and how, as fragments of the past return, with them come dark shadows that threaten to overwhelm her.

The book, *Children of Arnhem's Kaleidoscope*, is the story of the author's life in the Northern Territory: his childhood in an aboriginal community in remote Arnhem Land, in Australia's Northern Territory, of the people, danger and beauty of this place, and of its transformation over the last half century with the coming of aboriginal rights and the discovery or uranium. It also tells of his surviving an attack by a large crocodile and of his work over two decades in the outback of the NT.

Books are published as ebooks by Smashwords, Amazon, Kobo, Ibooks and other publishers. Some books are also available in print.

Graham is in the early stages of planning a memoir about his family's connections with Ireland called *Memories Only Remain* and also is compiling information for a book about the early NT cattle industry, its people and its stories.

Graham writes for the creative pleasure it brings him. He is particularly gratified each time an unknown person chooses to download and read something he has written and write a review - good or bad, as this gives him an insight into what readers enjoy and helps him make ongoing improvements to his writing.

In his other life Graham is a veterinarian who works in wildlife conservation and for rural landholders. He lived a large part of his life in the Northern Territory and his books reflect this experience.

Made in the USA
San Bernardino, CA
05 April 2017